The Eternal Forest

Fairy tales, Folk tales, Legends & Mythology, Volume 14

Patrick William Lee

Published by B&H Publishing Group, 2024.

THE ETERNAL FOREST

First edition. November 20, 2024.

Copyright © 2024 Patrick William Lee.

ISBN: 979-8227338259

Written by Patrick William Lee.

Table of Contents

Chapter 1: The Whispering Trees...1

Chapter 2: The Guardian of the Forest...8

Chapter 3: The First Encounter.. 16

Chapter 4: The Elusive Faeries.. 26

Chapter 5: The Sacred Grove... 33

Chapter 6: The Cursed Lake 40

Chapter 7: The Phoenix's Rebirth.. 50

Chapter 8: The Shadow of the Serpent.. 58

Chapter 9: The Hidden Village 66

Chapter 10: The Legend of the Eternal Flame 72

Chapter 11: The Trial of the Elements 81

Chapter 12: The Gathering of Creatures 89

Chapter 14: The Dawn of a New Era | Restoring Balance....................... 104

Chapter 15: The Legacy of the Eternal Forest... 111

To those who wander into the unknown,

seeking magic in the ordinary and legends in the whispers of the trees.

May you always find the courage to embrace the mysteries of the
world,

and the wisdom to protect its delicate balance.

This story is for the dreamers, the guardians,

and those who believe that even the quietest voices can change the
course of history.

For the forest within us all.

Chapter 1: The Whispering Trees

Introduction to the Eternal Forest

The sun was just beginning its descent, casting long shadows that stretched like fingers across the earth. A soft breeze stirred the leaves, causing them to rustle in a way that was almost musical. It was a sound that hinted at secrets, as if the trees themselves were trying to communicate with those who ventured close enough to listen. This was the edge of the Eternal Forest, a place shrouded in mystery, where time seemed to stand still and the boundaries between reality and myth blurred into one.

No one knew the true extent of the Eternal Forest. Some said it stretched across the entire continent, while others believed it was a place outside of time, existing only for those who were meant to find it. The trees, ancient and towering, stood like sentinels, their bark dark and gnarled, marked by the passage of countless centuries. Their roots twisted and coiled beneath the ground, a network of life that connected every part of the forest in ways unseen by the human eye.

It was here, at the forest's edge, that young Eamon stood, his heart pounding in his chest. He had heard the stories all his life—the tales of creatures that roamed these woods, of the Guardian who watched over them, and of the Whispering Trees that held the knowledge of ages. The forest was forbidden to the people of his village, a place of danger and wonder that none dared to enter. But Eamon was different. He had always felt the pull of the unknown, the call of the forest that seemed to sing to him in his dreams.

Eamon was not a large boy, nor particularly strong, but he was curious, and it was this curiosity that had led him to the edge of the Eternal Forest on this particular evening. His village lay behind him, a small cluster of houses surrounded by fields that had been tilled by generations of his ancestors. It was a simple life, one of hard work and quiet contentment, but for Eamon, it was not enough. He yearned for adventure, for something beyond the ordinary, and the Eternal Forest promised just that.

As he stood at the edge of the forest, the last rays of the sun filtering through the trees, Eamon felt a shiver of anticipation run down his spine. The forest was alive with sounds—the rustle of leaves, the chirping of unseen creatures, and, faintly, the whispering of the trees. It was a sound that seemed to come from all around him, a gentle murmur that grew louder the more he focused on it.

Taking a deep breath, Eamon stepped forward, crossing the threshold into the forest. The air seemed to change immediately, becoming cooler and filled with the rich, earthy scent of moss and damp leaves. The light dimmed as the canopy above him thickened, the branches intertwining to create a roof of greenery that blocked out much of the sky. He could feel the forest closing in around him, wrapping him in its embrace.

The path ahead was barely visible, more a suggestion of a trail than anything else, overgrown with ferns and wildflowers. Eamon moved cautiously, his eyes wide as he took in his surroundings. The trees were immense, their trunks so wide that it would take several men to encircle one with their arms. Their bark was rough to the touch, covered in patches of moss and lichen that added to their ancient appearance.

But it was the whispering that captivated Eamon the most. It was as if the trees were speaking to him, their voices soft and indistinct, like the murmuring of a crowd heard from a distance. He couldn't make out any specific words, but there was an undeniable sense of communication, as though the forest was trying to tell him something.

Eamon paused beside one of the largest trees, pressing his hand against its trunk. The bark was cool beneath his palm, and he closed his eyes, listening intently to the whispers. For a moment, he thought he could almost understand them, as if the meaning was just out of reach. The sound was soothing, a gentle hum that resonated deep within him, and he felt a strange sense of peace.

"Do you hear them?" A voice broke the silence, causing Eamon to startle and spin around.

Standing a few paces behind him was an old man, his hair white as snow and his beard long and unkempt. His eyes were bright, twinkling with a mischievous light, and he leaned on a gnarled wooden staff. He was dressed in simple robes, the fabric worn and faded, but there was an air of authority about him, a presence that made Eamon feel small in comparison.

"I... I think so," Eamon stammered, unsure of what to say. "The trees... they're whispering, aren't they?"

The old man nodded, a smile playing on his lips. "Aye, they are. The Whispering Trees, they call them. Not many can hear them, you know. It takes a special kind of person to truly listen."

Eamon's curiosity flared, and he took a step closer to the old man. "Who are you? And how do you know about the Whispering Trees?"

The old man chuckled, the sound deep and rumbling, like distant thunder. "Who I am is of little importance, lad. But as for the trees, well, I've been listening to them for longer than I care to remember. They speak of many things—the past, the present, and sometimes even the future. But they only share their secrets with those they deem worthy."

Eamon felt a thrill of excitement at the old man's words. "What do they say? Can you understand them?"

The old man tilted his head, his expression thoughtful. "Sometimes. They speak in riddles, mostly, and their words are not always easy to decipher. But if you listen closely, with your heart as well as your ears, you might catch a glimpse of the truth."

Eamon nodded, determined to understand the trees' whispers. He closed his eyes again, focusing all his attention on the sound. It was like trying to grasp smoke—intangible, elusive, but undeniably present. He could sense the trees' ancient wisdom, their knowledge of the world and all its secrets. But there was something more, something deeper, that he couldn't quite reach.

After a few moments, Eamon opened his eyes, frustrated by his inability to understand. "It's no use," he said, shaking his head. "I can't make sense of it."

The old man patted Eamon's shoulder kindly. "Don't be discouraged, lad. The forest is a place of mystery, and not all its secrets are meant to be uncovered at once. Patience is key. The trees have been here for thousands of years—they're in no hurry."

Eamon looked up at the towering trees, their branches swaying gently in the breeze. He knew the old man was right, but the desire to understand, to uncover the forest's secrets, burned within him. "Will you help me?" he asked, turning to the old man. "Will you teach me how to listen?"

The old man studied Eamon for a long moment, his eyes searching the boy's face. Finally, he nodded. "Very well. But know this, lad—once you start down this path, there's no turning back. The forest will change you, in ways you may not expect."

Eamon swallowed, feeling a mixture of excitement and trepidation. But he nodded, his resolve firm. "I'm ready."

The old man's smile widened, and he tapped his staff on the ground. "Then let us begin."

Together, they ventured deeper into the Eternal Forest, the trees' whispers growing louder as they walked. The path wound through the dense undergrowth, leading them into the heart of the woodland, where the trees stood even taller, their branches forming a nearly impenetrable canopy overhead. The light grew dimmer, the air cooler, and Eamon felt a sense of awe and reverence wash over him.

The old man led Eamon to a small clearing, where a circle of stones surrounded a large, flat rock. The ground was covered in a thick carpet of moss, and the air was filled with the scent of pine and earth. The old man gestured for Eamon to sit on the rock, and he did so, feeling the cool stone beneath him.

"This is a sacred place," the old man said, his voice soft. "The heart of the forest, where the Whispering Trees are strongest. Here, you can hear them more clearly, if you open yourself to their voices."

Eamon closed his eyes, taking a deep breath and letting it out slowly. He tried to calm his racing heart, focusing on the sounds around him. The whispering was louder now, more distinct, but still just beyond his understanding. He could feel the presence of the trees all around him, their roots deep in the earth, their branches reaching for the sky. It was as if the forest itself was alive, a single, vast entity that connected everything within it.

"Clear your mind," the old man instructed. "Let go of your thoughts, your doubts, and your fears. Let the forest speak to you, and listen with your heart."

Eamon did as he was told, pushing aside the worries and questions that crowded his mind. He focused on his breathing, the rise and fall of his chest, and the steady beat of his heart. Slowly, the world around him began to fade away, until there was nothing but the whispering of the trees.

At first, it was just a murmur, like the rustling of leaves in the wind. But gradually, the sound grew clearer, more distinct. Eamon could hear individual voices now, speaking in a language he couldn't understand, yet somehow, he knew what they were saying. It was as if the meaning was being transmitted directly into his mind, bypassing the need for words.

The voices spoke of many things—of the seasons that had come and gone, of the creatures that lived in the forest, and of the Guardian who watched over them all. They spoke of the forest's history, of the battles fought within its borders, and of the peace that had settled over it in recent years. But there was something else, something darker, lurking at the edges of the forest's consciousness. A sense of unease, of something not quite right.

Eamon's brow furrowed as he tried to grasp the meaning of the whispers. The voices grew louder, more insistent, but still, the message eluded him. He could feel the tension in the air, the sense that something was coming, something that could disrupt the delicate balance of the forest.

"Do you hear it?" the old man's voice broke through the whispers, pulling Eamon back to the present.

Eamon opened his eyes, blinking in the dim light. "I... I think so," he said slowly. "There's something wrong, isn't there? Something bad is coming."

The old man nodded, his expression grave. "The forest is worried, lad. It senses a disturbance, a threat to its peace. The trees are trying to warn us, to prepare us for what's to come."

Eamon felt a chill run down his spine. "What is it? What's going to happen?"

The old man shook his head. "I don't know. The trees speak in riddles, and their meaning is often unclear. But we must be vigilant, and we must be ready to protect the forest, whatever the cost."

Eamon looked around the clearing, at the towering trees that surrounded him. He had always thought of the forest as a place of safety, a refuge from the world outside. But now, he realized that it was also a place of great power, a power that could be both protective and destructive.

"What can we do?" he asked, his voice barely above a whisper.

The old man sighed, his shoulders sagging slightly. "We must listen, and we must learn. The forest will guide us, if we are willing to heed its warnings. But we must also be prepared to act, to defend the forest and all who dwell within it."

Eamon nodded, feeling the weight of responsibility settle on his shoulders. He had come to the forest seeking adventure, but now he realized that he had found something much more important—a purpose. The forest had chosen him, and he would do whatever it took to protect it.

For the rest of the day, Eamon and the old man sat in the clearing, listening to the whispers of the trees. The sun dipped lower in the sky, casting long shadows across the forest floor, but the air remained cool and still. The voices of the trees ebbed and flowed, sometimes clear and urgent, other times faint and indistinct.

As the first stars began to appear in the sky, the old man rose to his feet, tapping his staff on the ground. "It's time to go, lad. The forest has shared all it can for now."

Eamon stood as well, feeling a mixture of exhaustion and exhilaration. He had spent hours listening to the trees, trying to decipher their messages, and though he still had many questions, he felt a deep connection to the forest that he had never experienced before.

"Thank you," he said, turning to the old man. "For everything."

The old man smiled, a hint of sadness in his eyes. "You're welcome, lad. But this is just the beginning. The forest has much more to teach you, and there will be difficult days ahead. But remember—you're not alone. The forest will always be with you, as long as you listen."

With that, the old man began to walk back the way they had come, his steps slow and deliberate. Eamon followed, glancing back at the clearing one last time. The trees stood tall and silent, their whispers fading into the night. But Eamon knew that they were still there, watching and waiting, ready to share their secrets with those who were willing to listen.

As they made their way through the forest, the path seemed less daunting than before. The darkness was no longer oppressive, but comforting, like a blanket wrapped around him. Eamon felt a sense of belonging, of being part of something much larger than himself.

When they finally emerged from the forest, the village was quiet, the houses dark and still. Eamon could see the outline of his home in the distance, a small, familiar shape that seemed almost insignificant compared to the vastness of the forest. But he knew that it was his place in the world, the place where he would return to after every journey, every adventure.

"Remember, lad," the old man said, his voice soft in the night air. "The forest is a part of you now. It will guide you, protect you, but it will also test you. Be strong, be wise, and always listen to the whispers."

Eamon nodded, feeling a sense of determination settle in his chest. "I will. I promise."

The old man smiled, a faint glimmer of approval in his eyes. "Good. Now, go home and rest. Tomorrow is a new day, and the forest will have more to show you."

With a final nod, Eamon turned and made his way back to the village, his footsteps light on the dirt path. The old man watched him go, his expression unreadable, before turning back to the forest. The trees swayed gently in the breeze, their whispers barely audible, but the old man understood their message. The time of change was coming, and the boy would play a crucial role in the events that were about to unfold.

As the old man disappeared into the shadows of the forest, the trees resumed their whispering, their voices carrying on the wind. They spoke of the past, the present, and the future, their words weaving a tapestry of knowledge and power that only a few could truly comprehend. And in the heart of the Eternal Forest, where the ancient stones stood in silent vigil, a new chapter was about to begin—one that would test the strength of the forest, and the courage of those who called it home.

Chapter 2: The Guardian of the Forest

The Tale of the Ancient Protector

The Eternal Forest was more than just an expanse of trees and undergrowth. It was a living, breathing entity, a sanctuary for creatures of all kinds, from the smallest insects to the towering giants of legend. For millennia, this forest had stood as a testament to the power of nature, its secrets hidden deep within its heart. And at the center of it all was the Guardian—a creature as old as the forest itself, a being of immense wisdom and strength, whose sole purpose was to protect and maintain the balance of this sacred place.

Eamon awoke early the next morning, his mind still buzzing with the events of the previous day. The old man's words echoed in his thoughts as he dressed and prepared to venture back into the forest. He could still hear the faint whispers of the trees, a constant reminder of the mysteries he had only begun to uncover. But today, his thoughts were dominated by one thing: the Guardian.

The Guardian of the Forest was a figure of legend, spoken of in hushed tones by the elders of Eamon's village. Stories of the Guardian were passed down through generations, each tale more fantastical than the last. Some said the Guardian was a great beast, with eyes that glowed like the moon and claws sharp enough to cut through stone. Others claimed it was a spirit, formless and eternal, able to shift between the physical and ethereal realms at will. But no one knew the truth for certain, for the Guardian was rarely seen, and those who encountered it seldom spoke of it.

Eamon was determined to learn more. The old man had hinted at the Guardian's existence, and Eamon knew that if he was to understand the forest's secrets, he would need to understand the creature that protected it.

After a quick breakfast, Eamon made his way to the edge of the village, where the forest loomed like a vast, green wall. The sun was just beginning to rise, casting a soft, golden light over the treetops. The air was cool and crisp, and the forest was alive with the sounds of birds and insects greeting the new day.

Eamon hesitated for a moment at the forest's edge, taking a deep breath to steady his nerves. Then, with a final glance back at the village, he stepped into the shadows of the trees.

The path through the forest was familiar now, the landmarks recognizable after his journey the day before. But as he ventured deeper into the woods, the atmosphere began to change. The air grew cooler, and the light filtering through the canopy became dimmer, casting long shadows on the forest floor. The trees seemed to close in around him, their branches intertwining above to form a nearly impenetrable barrier.

Eamon felt a shiver run down his spine as he continued onward. The whispering of the trees was more pronounced here, their voices blending together in a constant murmur that filled the air. He couldn't make out any distinct words, but the sound was soothing, like a lullaby sung by the forest itself.

He had no clear destination in mind, but something deep within him seemed to guide his steps, leading him further into the heart of the forest. The path wound through dense undergrowth, past towering trees with gnarled roots that seemed to pulse with life. Eamon felt as though the forest was watching him, its presence all around him, unseen but undeniable.

After what felt like hours of walking, Eamon emerged into a small clearing. The ground here was covered in soft moss, and the trees formed a perfect circle around the space, their branches arching overhead to create a natural dome. In the center of the clearing stood a large stone, its surface smooth and weathered with age.

Eamon approached the stone cautiously, his heart pounding in his chest. The clearing had an otherworldly feel to it, as if it existed outside of time, untouched by the passage of years. The air was thick with the scent of pine and earth, and the whispering of the trees was louder here, their voices rising and falling in a rhythm that seemed almost musical.

As he reached the stone, Eamon noticed something carved into its surface. It was a symbol, simple yet intricate, made up of swirling lines and shapes that seemed to shift and change as he looked at them. He reached out to touch the carving, his fingers brushing against the cool stone.

The moment his hand made contact, the whispering of the trees grew louder, almost deafening, and Eamon felt a strange sensation wash over him.

It was as if the forest was reaching out to him, connecting with him on a level he couldn't fully comprehend. His vision blurred, and for a moment, the world around him seemed to dissolve into a swirling mass of light and sound.

When his vision cleared, Eamon found himself standing in the same clearing, but something was different. The light was dimmer, the shadows longer, and the air was thick with a sense of anticipation. He could feel a presence in the clearing, something vast and powerful, watching him from just beyond the edge of his perception.

"Who are you?" a voice rumbled through the air, deep and resonant, like the sound of distant thunder.

Eamon spun around, searching for the source of the voice, but there was no one there. The clearing was empty, save for the trees and the stone in the center.

"I... I'm Eamon," he stammered, his voice barely above a whisper. "I've come to learn about the forest... and about the Guardian."

There was a long pause, during which the only sound was the whispering of the trees. Then, the voice spoke again, this time softer, more measured.

"The Guardian... You seek knowledge of the Guardian?"

Eamon nodded, though he wasn't sure if the presence could see him. "Yes. I've heard the stories, but I want to know the truth. I want to understand."

The air in the clearing seemed to shift, as if the presence was considering his words. Then, with a sound like the rustling of leaves, the presence spoke once more.

"Very well. I will tell you the tale of the Guardian, for it is a tale as old as the forest itself. But know this, young one—knowledge comes with a price. Once you learn the truth, there is no going back."

Eamon swallowed, his heart racing. "I'm ready," he said, his voice firm despite the fear gnawing at him.

The presence seemed to approve of his resolve, for the air grew warmer, and the light in the clearing brightened slightly. The whispering of the trees grew softer, fading into the background as the voice began to speak.

"Long ago, before the first of your kind walked the earth, the Eternal Forest was born. It sprang from the heart of the world, a place of pure magic and life, untouched by the passage of time. The trees grew tall and strong, their roots digging deep into the earth, their branches reaching for the sky. The creatures of the forest thrived, living in harmony with the land and each other.

"But the forest was not without its dangers. There were forces in the world that sought to exploit the forest's power, to bend it to their will. Dark creatures, born of shadow and malice, sought to corrupt the forest, to twist its magic for their own purposes. And so, the Guardian was created—a being of immense power, charged with protecting the forest and maintaining the balance of life within it.

"The Guardian was not born, as you or I were born. It was shaped by the forest itself, a manifestation of its will and its magic. It took on a form that was both fearsome and wise, a reflection of the forest's strength and its ancient knowledge. The Guardian's purpose was clear: to defend the forest from any who would harm it, to ensure that the balance of life was never disrupted.

"For centuries, the Guardian watched over the forest, its presence a constant, silent sentinel. It kept the dark creatures at bay, driving them back into the shadows whenever they dared to encroach upon the forest's borders. The creatures of the forest revered the Guardian, for they knew that without it, the forest would fall into chaos.

"But as the ages passed, the Guardian began to change. It grew more aware of the world beyond the forest, of the creatures that lived in distant lands. It saw the rise and fall of empires, the birth and death of civilizations. And with this awareness came a new understanding—a realization that the balance of life extended beyond the forest, that the world itself was interconnected in ways that even the Guardian had not fully comprehended.

"This new understanding brought with it a great burden. The Guardian could no longer focus solely on the forest; it had to consider the world as a whole, to protect the balance of life on a grander scale. But this was no easy task, for the world was vast and complex, and the forces that threatened it were numerous and powerful.

"And so, the Guardian made a choice—a choice that would forever change its role and its connection to the forest. It chose to bind itself to the very heart of the forest, to become one with the land and the trees. In doing so, the Guardian's power was amplified, allowing it to reach beyond the borders of the forest, to sense disturbances in the balance of life no matter where they occurred.

"But this binding came with a cost. The Guardian could no longer take physical form, could no longer walk the forest as it once had. It became a presence, a consciousness that permeated every inch of the forest, a voice that could only be heard by those who were truly attuned to the forest's magic. The Guardian's connection to the forest was now absolute, but it was also isolated, separated from the world it sought to protect.

"Over the centuries, the Guardian has watched as the world has changed, as new threats have arisen and old ones have faded away. It has seen the coming of your kind, the humans, and has observed with both hope and fear the impact you have had on the world. The Guardian knows that the balance of life is more fragile than ever, and it remains vigilant, ready to act should the need arise.

"But the Guardian is not infallible. It is powerful, yes, but it is also bound by the limitations of its existence. It cannot intervene directly in the affairs of the world, for to do so would disrupt the very balance it seeks to protect. Instead, it must rely on those who are willing to listen, to learn, and to act on its behalf. It must trust in the wisdom and the courage of those who walk the path of the forest, just as you have chosen to do."

As the voice finished speaking, the clearing fell silent. The whispering of the trees had ceased entirely, leaving only the soft rustle of leaves in the breeze. Eamon stood in the center of the clearing, his mind racing as he tried to process everything he had just heard.

The Guardian was more than just a creature of legend—it was the very essence of the forest, a being of unimaginable power and responsibility. And now, Eamon understood why the old man had brought him here, why he had been chosen to listen to the trees. The forest needed him, just as it needed others like him, to help protect the balance of life.

But with this understanding came a deep sense of fear. How could he, a simple boy from a small village, possibly live up to the expectations of the Guardian? How could he protect something so vast, so ancient, when he barely understood it himself?

As if sensing his doubts, the voice spoke again, this time with a gentleness that surprised Eamon.

"Do not be afraid, young one. The path before you is difficult, yes, but you are not alone. The forest is with you, and the Guardian will guide you. Trust in yourself, and in the wisdom of the trees. You have the strength within you to do what must be done."

Eamon took a deep breath, letting the words wash over him. The fear was still there, a nagging doubt that he couldn't quite shake, but it was tempered by a newfound determination. He had made a promise to the old man, and now he had made a promise to the forest as well. He would not back down, no matter how daunting the task ahead.

With renewed resolve, Eamon turned his attention back to the stone in the center of the clearing. The symbol carved into its surface seemed to glow faintly, as if it were alive with the magic of the forest. Eamon reached out to touch it once more, and as his fingers brushed against the stone, he felt a surge of energy course through him.

In that moment, Eamon knew that he was connected to the forest in a way he had never been before. He could feel its life force flowing through him, could sense the presence of the Guardian all around him. The whispers of the trees returned, but this time they were clear, their voices harmonizing in a chorus that resonated deep within his soul.

The Guardian was with him, and he with the Guardian. Together, they would protect the forest, and the balance of life that depended on it.

Eamon stood in the clearing for a long time, his hand resting on the stone as he listened to the whispers of the trees. The sun had risen higher in the sky, casting dappled light across the forest floor, but the air remained cool and calm. The forest felt alive, vibrant with the energy of countless beings, all connected by the unseen threads of life.

Finally, Eamon released the stone and stepped back, his heart pounding with a mixture of excitement and trepidation. He had come to the forest seeking adventure, but what he had found was something far greater—a purpose, a calling that would shape the course of his life.

But as he turned to leave the clearing, to return to the village and the life he had known, a thought occurred to him. The Guardian had spoken of the balance of life, of the need to protect it not just within the forest, but in the world beyond. What if the disturbances the Guardian had sensed were not confined to the forest? What if the threats to the balance of life extended to the human world as well?

Eamon's brow furrowed as he considered the implications. The forest was vast, but the world was even larger, filled with countless people and creatures, all interconnected in ways that were both complex and fragile. If the balance of life was disrupted, the consequences could be catastrophic, not just for the forest, but for the entire world.

The thought filled Eamon with a sense of urgency. He could not wait for the threats to reveal themselves—he needed to be proactive, to seek out the disturbances and address them before it was too late. But where to begin? The world was so vast, and Eamon was just one person. How could he possibly make a difference?

As if in response to his thoughts, the whispering of the trees grew louder, more insistent. Eamon closed his eyes, focusing on the voices, letting them guide him. The trees spoke of distant lands, of places where the balance of life was already beginning to fray. They spoke of dark creatures lurking in the shadows, of forces that sought to unravel the delicate threads that held the world together.

But they also spoke of hope, of allies who could help Eamon in his quest. The Guardian was not the only protector of the balance of life—there were others, scattered across the world, who shared its purpose and its mission. If Eamon could find them, he would not have to face the challenges ahead alone.

Eamon's heart swelled with determination. He would not rest until he had done everything in his power to protect the balance of life, to preserve the harmony that the Guardian and the forest had worked so hard to maintain. He would seek out the allies the trees had spoken of, and together, they would stand against the forces of darkness that threatened the world.

With a final look at the clearing, Eamon turned and began the journey back to the village. The path ahead was uncertain, and the challenges he would face were daunting, but he knew that he could not turn back now. The forest had chosen him, and he would honor that choice with every step he took.

As he walked, the whispering of the trees followed him, a constant reminder of the task that lay ahead. The Guardian's presence was with him as well, a silent sentinel that would guide him in the days to come. Eamon felt a sense of peace, knowing that he was not alone, that the forest and the Guardian would be with him every step of the way.

But even as he left the forest behind and the village came into view, Eamon knew that this was only the beginning. The journey ahead would be long and difficult, filled with dangers and trials that would test his resolve. But he was ready, and he would face whatever came his way with the strength and wisdom that the forest had bestowed upon him.

And so, as the sun climbed higher in the sky and the day began in earnest, Eamon made his way home, his heart filled with a new sense of purpose. The balance of life depended on him, and he would not rest until he had done everything in his power to protect it.

The Guardian of the Forest had entrusted him with this sacred duty, and Eamon would not let it down. The journey ahead was uncertain, but one thing was clear—Eamon would do whatever it took to ensure that the balance of life was preserved, not just for the forest, but for the entire world.

Chapter 3: The First Encounter

A Traveler's Journey into the Unknown

The road had been long, winding through the rolling hills and fertile valleys of the land, until it finally gave way to the untamed wilderness that lay at the borders of the Eternal Forest. From here, the well-worn path faded into the dense undergrowth, swallowed by the towering trees that marked the edge of this ancient and mysterious place. The young traveler stood at the forest's edge, staring into the darkness beneath the canopy, where the sunlight struggled to penetrate and the shadows danced with a life of their own.

His name was Finnian, but most called him Finn. He was a youth of twenty summers, with a lean frame hardened by years of wandering, and bright, inquisitive eyes that gleamed with a mixture of curiosity and determination. His sandy hair was tied back in a simple knot, and he wore the practical garb of a traveler—a sturdy tunic, worn boots, and a weathered cloak that had seen many miles. A leather satchel hung at his side, filled with the few possessions he carried with him on his journeys.

Finn had heard the stories of the Eternal Forest for as long as he could remember. Tales of a place where time itself seemed to stand still, where the trees whispered secrets to those who would listen, and where creatures of legend roamed free, untouched by the passage of ages. It was a place of wonder and danger, a place that few dared to enter and even fewer returned from. But for Finn, it was a place of opportunity—a chance to prove himself, to uncover the mysteries that lay hidden within, and to forge his own destiny.

He had traveled for weeks to reach this point, following the rumors and stories that had led him to the very edge of the Eternal Forest. Now, as he stood before the towering trees that marked the boundary between the world he knew and the unknown, he felt a thrill of anticipation course through him. This was it—the moment he had been waiting for.

Taking a deep breath, Finn adjusted the strap of his satchel and stepped forward, crossing the threshold into the forest. The change was immediate. The air grew cooler, thick with the scent of moss and earth, and the sounds of the outside world—the chirping of birds, the rustling of leaves in the wind—faded into silence. The only sound now was the soft crunch of his boots on the forest floor and the distant murmur of the trees, their whispers barely audible above the sound of his own heartbeat.

Finn paused for a moment, taking in his surroundings. The trees here were immense, their trunks wide and gnarled, their branches reaching high into the sky. The canopy overhead was so thick that it blocked out most of the sunlight, casting the forest in a perpetual twilight. The undergrowth was dense, filled with ferns and shrubs, and the path ahead was barely discernible, more a suggestion of a trail than an actual road.

Undeterred, Finn pressed on, moving deeper into the forest. He had no map, no guide to show him the way, but he trusted his instincts and the stories he had heard. The forest was a place of magic, and magic had a way of guiding those who were meant to find it.

As he walked, the forest seemed to close in around him, the trees growing taller and the shadows deeper. The whispering of the trees grew louder, more distinct, but still, the words were just out of reach, like a conversation overheard from a distance. Finn strained to listen, but the meaning eluded him, leaving him with only a sense of unease.

Hours passed, though it was difficult to tell time in the Eternal Forest. The light remained dim, the air cool and still, and the forest itself seemed to pulse with a life of its own. Finn could feel it in the ground beneath his feet, in the rustle of the leaves overhead, in the very air he breathed. The forest was alive, aware of his presence, and it was watching him.

Despite the eerie atmosphere, Finn's resolve never wavered. He had come to the Eternal Forest with a purpose, and he would not be deterred by shadows or whispers. He pushed forward, his steps sure and steady, his eyes scanning the forest for any sign of the creatures that were said to dwell within.

It wasn't long before he encountered his first sign of life. A flicker of movement caught his eye, and he turned just in time to see a small, deer-like creature dart between the trees. It was no ordinary deer, however. Its coat was a deep, iridescent blue, shimmering like the surface of a lake at twilight, and its antlers were delicate and silver, branching out like the limbs of a tree. The creature paused for a moment, turning its large, luminous eyes toward Finn, and he felt a jolt of recognition—it was a faun, a creature of legend, said to be one of the forest's guardians.

For a moment, Finn and the faun simply stared at each other, the air between them thick with an unspoken understanding. Then, with a flick of its tail, the faun bounded away, disappearing into the shadows as quickly as it had appeared. Finn stood still, his heart pounding in his chest. He had seen many strange and wondrous things in his travels, but nothing quite like this. The sight of the faun filled him with a sense of awe, a reminder that he was in a place where the ordinary rules of the world did not apply.

As he continued on, Finn encountered more of the forest's inhabitants—creatures that existed only in the pages of old tales and the memories of the oldest storytellers. He saw a flock of birds with feathers that glowed like embers, flitting through the trees in a burst of fiery color. He caught a glimpse of a great wolf, its fur as white as snow, its eyes as dark as night, watching him from the shadows with a gaze that seemed to pierce his very soul. And once, he even thought he saw a dragon—a massive, serpentine creature with scales that glimmered like polished metal, soaring high above the canopy with a grace that belied its size.

Each encounter left Finn more convinced that he had found what he was looking for. The Eternal Forest was a place of magic, a place where the old stories came to life and the impossible became reality. But it was also a place of danger, and Finn knew that he could not afford to let his guard down. The creatures he had seen were beautiful, yes, but they were also powerful, and he had no doubt that they could be deadly if provoked.

As the day wore on, Finn found himself growing weary. The forest was vast, and though he had been walking for hours, he had no sense of how far he had come or how much farther he had to go. The light remained dim, the shadows deepening as the sun began its descent, though Finn could not see the sky through the thick canopy overhead. He knew he would need to find a place to rest soon, a safe spot where he could set up camp for the night.

His thoughts were interrupted by a sudden rustling in the undergrowth ahead. Finn froze, his hand instinctively going to the hilt of the dagger at his belt. The sound grew louder, closer, and Finn's heart began to race. He had encountered many creatures in the forest, but none had approached him directly. Whatever was making the noise was coming toward him, and it was doing so with purpose.

The rustling stopped, and for a moment, there was silence. Finn strained his ears, every muscle in his body tensed, ready to spring into action. Then, with a burst of movement, something shot out of the undergrowth, heading straight for him.

Finn barely had time to react. He leapt to the side, narrowly avoiding the creature as it lunged at him. He spun around, drawing his dagger as he did so, and faced his attacker.

It was unlike anything he had ever seen. The creature was small, no larger than a dog, with a lithe, serpentine body covered in shimmering green scales. Its eyes were large and bright, glowing with an inner light, and its mouth was filled with sharp, needle-like teeth. It moved with incredible speed, darting back and forth, its movements fluid and almost hypnotic.

The creature hissed, baring its teeth as it circled Finn, clearly preparing to strike again. Finn tightened his grip on his dagger, his mind racing as he tried to remember everything he had heard about the creatures of the Eternal Forest. This one was unfamiliar to him—none of the stories had mentioned anything like it. But one thing was clear: it was a predator, and it had chosen him as its prey.

The creature lunged again, faster this time, its jaws snapping at Finn's leg. Finn barely managed to dodge, rolling to the side and coming up in a crouch, his dagger held defensively in front of him. The creature hissed in frustration, its eyes narrowing as it prepared for another attack.

Finn knew he couldn't keep dodging forever. He needed to find a way to either scare the creature off or defeat it, and he needed to do it quickly. He glanced around, searching for anything he could use to his advantage, but the forest offered little in the way of weapons or cover. The creature was too fast, too agile—it would wear him down eventually if he didn't do something.

Desperation fueled his thoughts, and in a split second, an idea formed in his mind. It was risky, but it might just work. Finn steadied himself, waiting for the creature to make its move. He knew it would come at him again, and this time, he would be ready.

The creature hissed once more, its body coiling like a spring. Then, with a burst of speed, it shot toward Finn, its jaws wide open, aiming for his throat.

But Finn was ready. He waited until the last possible moment, then threw himself to the ground, rolling onto his back as the creature sailed over him. In one swift motion, he brought his dagger up, slicing through the air with all his strength.

The blade connected with the creature's underbelly, and there was a sharp, high-pitched screech as the creature veered off course, crashing into the undergrowth. Finn scrambled to his feet, breathing hard, his dagger held out in front of him. The creature lay on the ground a few feet away, writhing in pain, its bright eyes dimming as it bled out from the wound Finn had inflicted.

Finn didn't hesitate. He rushed forward, plunging his dagger into the creature's neck, putting an end to its suffering. The creature went still, its body going limp as its life drained away.

For a moment, Finn just stood there, staring down at the creature's lifeless form, his breath coming in ragged gasps. The reality of what had just happened began to sink in—he had faced down a predator, a creature unlike anything he had ever encountered, and he had survived. But the victory felt hollow, tainted by the knowledge that the creature had been acting on instinct, defending its territory against an intruder.

Finn knelt beside the creature, examining it more closely now that it was no longer a threat. It was beautiful in its own way, its scales shimmering like emeralds, its form sleek and perfectly adapted to its environment. Finn couldn't help but feel a pang of regret as he looked at it—regret that it had come to this, that he had been forced to take a life in this place of wonder.

But there was no time for mourning. The forest was still alive with dangers, and Finn knew he needed to find shelter before nightfall. He wiped his dagger clean on the grass, then sheathed it, rising to his feet. With one last glance at the fallen creature, he turned and continued on his way, his senses alert for any sign of further danger.

The light continued to fade as Finn pressed deeper into the forest. The trees grew closer together, their branches forming a tangled web overhead, and the undergrowth became thicker, more difficult to navigate. The forest seemed to pulse with life, but it was a life that was alien to Finn, filled with creatures and plants that defied explanation.

Just as he was beginning to lose hope of finding a suitable place to rest, Finn stumbled upon a small clearing. It was a perfect circle, the ground covered in soft moss, with a large, flat rock at its center. The rock was smooth and cool to the touch, and Finn could see faint markings on its surface, worn away by time but still visible in the dim light.

Finn knew instinctively that this was no ordinary clearing. There was a sense of peace here, a feeling that this place was somehow protected from the dangers of the forest. He couldn't explain it, but he felt safe, as if the very air around him was offering shelter.

He set down his satchel and began to prepare a small camp. He gathered some fallen branches and dry leaves, arranging them into a makeshift fire pit on the rock. With a few strikes of his flint, he managed to coax a small flame to life, the fire crackling softly as it grew. The light from the fire cast a warm glow over the clearing, pushing back the shadows that had gathered around him.

As the fire burned, Finn sat back against the rock, letting out a long sigh of relief. He had made it through the first day, and though the journey had been fraught with danger, he was still alive. But the forest had only just begun to reveal its secrets, and Finn knew that there were many more challenges ahead.

The firelight danced on the leaves overhead, casting flickering shadows on the ground. The whispering of the trees had returned, a constant murmur that filled the clearing with a sense of life and energy. Finn closed his eyes, letting the sound wash over him, his mind drifting as the exhaustion of the day began to catch up with him.

As he sat there, on the edge of sleep, Finn heard something—a faint sound, almost like a melody, carried on the breeze. He opened his eyes, listening intently, but the sound was elusive, slipping away before he could grasp it. It was like the whispering of the trees, but different—more deliberate, more purposeful.

Finn stood, scanning the clearing for any sign of movement. The fire crackled softly, the shadows flickering in the light, but there was nothing else—no creatures, no danger. Just the faint, haunting melody that seemed to come from everywhere and nowhere at once.

Intrigued, Finn stepped away from the fire, moving toward the edge of the clearing. The melody grew louder, more distinct, and Finn realized that it was coming from somewhere deep within the forest. It was a beautiful sound, haunting and ethereal, like the song of a nightingale, but with an otherworldly quality that sent a shiver down his spine.

Without thinking, Finn began to follow the sound, his feet moving of their own accord as he was drawn toward the source of the melody. The forest around him grew darker, the shadows deeper, but the sound was a beacon, guiding him through the tangled undergrowth.

He wasn't sure how far he had walked—time seemed to lose all meaning in the Eternal Forest—but eventually, the trees began to thin, and Finn found himself standing at the edge of another clearing. This one was larger than the first, the ground covered in soft, glowing flowers that bathed the clearing in a soft, golden light.

And in the center of the clearing stood a figure.

At first, Finn thought it was a woman, her form slender and graceful, her long hair flowing like a river of silver. But as he drew closer, he realized that this was no ordinary woman. Her skin was pale, almost translucent, and her eyes glowed with the same golden light as the flowers. She wore a gown of flowing fabric that seemed to shimmer and change color with every movement, and around her head was a crown of delicate, iridescent feathers.

The melody that had drawn Finn to the clearing was coming from her, her voice rising and falling in a song that seemed to resonate with the very air around her. It was a sound that was both beautiful and unsettling, a melody that spoke of longing and loss, of love and sorrow.

Finn stood at the edge of the clearing, captivated by the sight before him. He knew instinctively that this was no ordinary being—she was a creature of magic, a spirit of the forest, and her presence filled the clearing with a sense of power and wonder.

The spirit continued to sing, her voice weaving through the air like a thread, drawing Finn closer. He took a step forward, then another, until he was standing just a few feet from her, his breath catching in his throat.

As if sensing his presence, the spirit's song trailed off, and she turned her glowing eyes toward him. For a moment, there was silence, the air between them heavy with unspoken words. Then, in a voice that was as soft as a whisper, she spoke.

"Who are you, traveler?"

Finn swallowed, his throat suddenly dry. "My name is Finn," he said, his voice barely above a whisper. "I've come to explore the Eternal Forest, to uncover its secrets."

The spirit tilted her head, her gaze piercing as she studied him. "You are brave to venture into these woods, Finn. Few have the courage to do so."

Finn nodded, though he wasn't sure if it was bravery or foolishness that had driven him to this point. "I've heard the stories, the legends. I wanted to see if they were true."

The spirit's lips curved into a faint smile. "The stories hold a grain of truth, but the reality is far more complex. The Eternal Forest is a place of great power, but also of great danger. You must be careful, Finn, for not all who enter these woods leave unscathed."

"I know the risks," Finn said, his voice steadier now. "But I'm willing to take them. I want to learn, to understand."

The spirit's smile faded, her expression turning somber. "Understanding comes at a cost, traveler. The more you learn, the more you will be changed. The forest does not reveal its secrets lightly, and those who seek them must be prepared to pay the price."

Finn hesitated, the weight of her words sinking in. He had known that this journey would be dangerous, that the forest was a place of mystery and magic, but hearing it from the spirit herself made it all the more real. He was not just an explorer, a traveler on a quest—he was a participant in something much larger, something that could change him in ways he couldn't yet comprehend.

But despite the fear that gnawed at him, Finn knew that he couldn't turn back now. He had come too far, seen too much, to walk away. Whatever the cost, he was willing to pay it.

"I understand," Finn said, his voice firm. "I'm ready."

The spirit studied him for a long moment, her glowing eyes searching his face as if looking for something hidden deep within him. Then, with a nod, she seemed to come to a decision.

"Very well, Finn," she said softly. "You have chosen your path, and I will not stand in your way. But know this—the forest is watching you, and it will test you. Be strong, be wise, and trust in the magic that flows through these woods. It will guide you, if you are willing to listen."

Finn nodded, feeling a mixture of relief and trepidation. The spirit's words were both a warning and a blessing, and he knew that he would need to heed them carefully if he was to survive the trials that lay ahead.

The spirit turned away, her gaze sweeping over the clearing as she raised her arms, the sleeves of her gown billowing like the wings of a bird. The flowers at her feet began to glow brighter, their light spreading through the clearing like a wave, and the air was filled with the soft hum of magic.

As Finn watched, the spirit's form began to change, her body dissolving into the light, until she was nothing more than a shimmering mist that drifted through the clearing like a wisp of smoke. The flowers continued to glow, their light pulsing with a gentle rhythm, but the spirit herself was gone, leaving only the memory of her presence behind.

Finn stood in the clearing for a long time, his mind reeling from the encounter. He had come to the forest seeking adventure, but what he had found was something far more profound—a connection to a world of magic and wonder that he had only ever dreamed of. The spirit's words echoed in his mind, a reminder that his journey was only just beginning, and that the true challenges still lay ahead.

As the light from the flowers began to fade, Finn turned and made his way back to his camp. The forest was still alive with whispers, but they no longer filled him with unease—instead, they seemed to guide him, to offer him comfort in the darkness.

When he reached the clearing where his fire still burned, Finn sat down beside the flames, staring into the flickering light as he replayed the events of the day in his mind. The encounter with the spirit had shaken him, but it had also filled him with a sense of purpose, a determination to see his journey through to the end.

He knew that the road ahead would be difficult, that the forest would test him in ways he couldn't yet imagine. But he also knew that he was not alone—the spirit, the forest, and the magic that flowed through it all would be with him every step of the way.

With that thought in mind, Finn lay back on the soft moss, his eyes growing heavy as sleep began to overtake him. The fire crackled softly, the trees whispered their secrets, and the Eternal Forest watched over him as he drifted off into the world of dreams, where the magic of the forest would continue to weave its spell.

And so, the young traveler's journey into the unknown had truly begun, a journey that would take him to the very heart of the Eternal Forest and beyond, to places where few had ventured and fewer still had returned. But Finn was ready, for he had chosen his path, and there was no turning back.

The adventure of a lifetime awaited him, filled with wonders and dangers beyond his wildest imagination. And though he did not yet know it, Finn's first encounter with the spirit of the forest was only the beginning of a tale that would change him—and the world—forever.

Chapter 4: The Elusive Faeries

Meeting the Forest's Playful Spirits

The Eternal Forest was a place where magic thrived, and where the boundaries between reality and myth blurred into one. Finnian, or Finn as he was known, had already encountered creatures of legend within these ancient woods. He had met the Guardian, a being of immense power and wisdom, and had felt the weight of responsibility that now rested upon his shoulders. But despite the challenges he had faced, Finn's curiosity remained undiminished. He knew that the forest had many more secrets to reveal, and he was determined to uncover them all.

The morning after his encounter with the forest spirit, Finn awoke to the gentle sound of birdsong. The clearing where he had made camp was bathed in soft, golden light, the dew glistening on the moss-covered ground. The fire had long since died down, leaving only a few smoldering embers, but the air was warm and filled with the earthy scent of the forest.

Finn stretched and yawned, feeling the stiffness in his muscles from the previous day's exertions. He had slept deeply, his dreams filled with images of the forest and its many inhabitants. But now, as he sat up and looked around, he felt a renewed sense of purpose. The spirit's words still echoed in his mind, a reminder that the forest was watching him, and that his journey was far from over.

After a quick breakfast of dried fruit and bread, Finn packed up his belongings and set out once more. He had no clear destination in mind, but he trusted that the forest would guide him, as it had before. The path ahead was uncertain, but that was part of the adventure—part of the reason he had come to the Eternal Forest in the first place.

As he walked, Finn found himself reflecting on the creatures he had already encountered. The faun, the glowing birds, the great white wolf—each had been a marvel in its own right, a living testament to the magic that permeated the forest. But there was one group of beings he had yet to encounter, though he had heard many stories about them: the faeries.

The faeries of the Eternal Forest were said to be among the most elusive of its inhabitants. Tiny yet powerful, they were known for their playful and mischievous nature, often leading travelers astray or playing tricks on those who ventured too close to their hidden groves. But they were also wise, possessing knowledge of the forest that few others could claim. Finn had heard that the faeries could reveal secrets, offer cryptic advice, and even alter the course of a person's fate—if they were in the mood to do so.

The thought of meeting the faeries filled Finn with both excitement and apprehension. He had always been fascinated by tales of these magical beings, but he also knew that they could be dangerous if provoked. The faeries were not bound by the same rules as humans—they lived by their own code, and those who did not respect their ways often found themselves at their mercy.

As he walked deeper into the forest, the trees grew taller and the undergrowth thicker. The air was cooler here, the light dimmer, and the whispering of the trees was more pronounced, as if they were trying to warn him of something. Finn kept his senses alert, his eyes scanning the path ahead for any sign of movement. He knew that the faeries could be anywhere, watching him from the shadows, waiting for the right moment to reveal themselves.

Hours passed, and the forest remained quiet, save for the occasional rustle of leaves or the chirping of birds. Finn began to wonder if he would ever find the faeries—if they even wanted to be found. He had heard that they were capricious, appearing only when it suited them, and that they often chose to remain hidden from those who sought them out.

But just as he was beginning to lose hope, something caught his eye. A flicker of movement, so quick and subtle that he almost missed it. Finn paused, his heart skipping a beat as he scanned the area. There it was again—a tiny flash of light, like the glint of sunlight on water, darting between the trees.

Finn held his breath, not wanting to startle whatever it was that had caught his attention. Slowly, he began to move toward the light, his footsteps careful and deliberate. The light danced ahead of him, flitting from tree to tree, its movements graceful and fluid. It seemed to be leading him somewhere, guiding him deeper into the forest.

The trees began to thin, and soon Finn found himself standing at the edge of a small glade. The grass here was a vibrant green, dotted with wildflowers of every color, and the air was filled with the sweet scent of blooming flowers. But it was the light that held Finn's attention—the same light that had led him here, now hovering in the center of the glade like a tiny, glowing orb.

As Finn watched, the light began to change, growing brighter and more intense until it was almost blinding. He shielded his eyes, squinting against the glare, and when the light finally dimmed, he saw that the orb had transformed into a small figure—no more than a foot tall, with delicate wings that shimmered in the sunlight.

It was a faerie.

The faerie hovered in the air, its wings beating rapidly, creating a soft, buzzing sound. Its features were sharp and angular, with large, almond-shaped eyes that glowed with an inner light. Its skin was a pale, silvery hue, and its hair, which flowed down its back in a cascade of shimmering strands, seemed to shift colors with every movement.

For a moment, Finn was too stunned to speak. He had never seen anything like it—this creature of legend, now hovering before him, was more beautiful and ethereal than he could have ever imagined. The faerie regarded him with a curious expression, its eyes narrowing as if assessing whether he was friend or foe.

Finally, Finn found his voice. "Hello," he said, his voice barely above a whisper. "Are you... are you one of the faeries?"

The faerie tilted its head to one side, as if considering his question. Then, with a flick of its wings, it darted forward, stopping just inches from Finn's face. Finn held his breath, trying not to move, as the faerie studied him up close. Its eyes were filled with a strange intelligence, as if it could see right through him, into the very depths of his soul.

After what felt like an eternity, the faerie pulled back, hovering at eye level with Finn. "I am," it said, its voice high-pitched and melodic, like the tinkling of a bell. "And you are a traveler, are you not? One who seeks the secrets of the forest?"

Finn nodded, still trying to process the fact that he was speaking to a faerie. "Yes," he replied. "I've come to learn about the Eternal Forest, to understand its magic."

The faerie's lips curled into a mischievous smile. "Many have sought to understand the forest's magic, but few have succeeded. The forest is a place of mystery, and its secrets are not easily given."

"I know," Finn said, his voice earnest. "But I'm willing to try. I want to learn, to understand."

The faerie regarded him for a long moment, its expression unreadable. Then, with a nod, it gestured for Finn to follow. "Come," it said, its voice light and airy. "There is much to see, much to learn. But be warned, traveler—what you seek may not be what you find."

With that cryptic remark, the faerie turned and flew off, darting across the glade with the speed and agility of a hummingbird. Finn hesitated for only a moment before hurrying after it, his heart pounding with excitement and anticipation.

The faerie led him through the glade and into the forest beyond, where the trees grew tall and the undergrowth was thick and tangled. Finn had to duck and weave to avoid getting caught on the branches, but the faerie moved effortlessly, its wings barely brushing the leaves as it flew.

They traveled for what felt like miles, the faerie weaving through the forest with a speed and grace that left Finn breathless. He had never seen anyone move like this, and he struggled to keep up, his legs burning with the effort. But the faerie never slowed, never faltered, as if it was a part of the forest itself, moving with the rhythm of the trees and the wind.

Finally, they reached another clearing, this one larger and more open than the last. The trees here were spaced farther apart, allowing beams of sunlight to filter down through the canopy and bathe the ground in a warm, golden light. The air was filled with the hum of insects and the soft rustling of leaves, and the grass was a vibrant green, dotted with wildflowers that seemed to glow in the light.

But it was what lay at the center of the clearing that caught Finn's attention. A large, ancient oak tree stood there, its gnarled roots twisting and coiling around the base like the tendrils of some great beast. The tree's bark was dark and weathered, and its branches stretched high into the sky, forming a dense canopy overhead.

At the base of the tree, nestled among the roots, was a small, glowing pool of water. The water was clear and still, reflecting the sunlight like a mirror, and the air around it seemed to shimmer with magic.

The faerie hovered beside the pool, its wings beating softly as it watched Finn approach. "This is the Heart of the Forest," it said, its voice reverent. "A place of great power, where the magic of the forest is strongest.

It is here that the faeries gather, where we draw our strength and our wisdom."

Finn stared at the pool, mesmerized by its beauty. He could feel the magic in the air, a tangible presence that seemed to hum in his veins. It was unlike anything he had ever experienced—a raw, untamed power that filled him with awe and wonder.

As he knelt beside the pool, the faerie fluttered down to land on a nearby root, its wings folding neatly against its back. "The Heart of the Forest has existed for as long as the forest itself," it said, its voice soft. "It is a place of creation and renewal, where the magic of the forest is born and reborn with each passing season. The faeries are its guardians, its protectors, and it is our duty to ensure that the balance of the forest is maintained."

Finn looked up at the faerie, his curiosity piqued. "The balance of the forest? What do you mean?"

The faerie's eyes gleamed with a knowing light. "The forest is a living entity, a vast and complex web of life that is connected in ways you cannot yet comprehend. Every creature, every plant, every stone and stream is part of this web, and the balance of life within the forest is delicate. If one part of the web is disturbed, it can have consequences for the entire forest."

Finn nodded, absorbing the faerie's words. He had always known that the forest was a place of magic, but he had never considered the idea of balance, of the interconnectedness of all things within it. It was a humbling thought, and it made him realize just how little he truly understood about the world he had entered.

The faerie seemed to sense his thoughts, for it smiled and said, "Do not be discouraged, traveler. Understanding the forest is not something that happens overnight. It takes time, patience, and a willingness to listen. The forest speaks in many voices, and only those who are truly attuned to its magic can hear them all."

Finn looked down at the pool, his reflection staring back at him from the still surface of the water. He could see the uncertainty in his own eyes, the doubt that had begun to creep in. But he could also see the determination, the resolve that had brought him to this point.

"I want to learn," Finn said quietly. "I want to understand the forest, to understand its magic. But I don't know where to start."

The faerie fluttered its wings, lifting off the root and hovering in front of Finn. "The forest is your teacher, traveler," it said, its voice filled with a wisdom beyond its years. "It will guide you, if you are willing to listen. But remember—understanding comes at a cost. The more you learn, the more you will be changed. The forest will test you, and you must be prepared to face those tests with courage and humility."

Finn nodded, his heart filled with a mixture of fear and excitement. He knew that the road ahead would be difficult, that the forest would challenge him in ways he couldn't yet imagine. But he also knew that he couldn't turn back now. He had come too far, seen too much, to walk away.

"Thank you," Finn said, his voice sincere. "Thank you for your guidance."

The faerie smiled, a twinkle of mischief in its eyes. "Do not thank me just yet, traveler. The forest has many more secrets to reveal, and not all of them are pleasant. But if you are true of heart, if you are willing to face the challenges ahead, then you may just find what you seek."

With those words, the faerie began to glow brighter, its form shimmering with an inner light. Finn watched in awe as the faerie's wings grew larger, its body stretching and elongating until it was no longer a tiny, delicate creature, but a towering, majestic figure, its wings spanning the entire clearing.

The light grew brighter and brighter, until Finn was forced to shield his eyes. He could feel the magic in the air, a powerful, overwhelming force that filled every corner of the clearing. And then, just as suddenly as it had begun, the light dimmed, and the faerie was gone.

Finn blinked, his vision slowly returning to normal. The clearing was quiet, the only sound the soft rustling of leaves in the breeze. The pool at the base of the tree was still there, its surface as smooth and reflective as ever, but the faerie had vanished, leaving Finn alone with his thoughts.

He sat there for a long time, staring into the pool, his mind racing with everything that had just happened. The faerie had spoken of balance, of the interconnectedness of all things within the forest, and Finn knew that this was a lesson he would need to take to heart if he was to survive in this place.

But the faerie had also spoken of tests, of challenges that he would need to face. Finn didn't know what those tests would be, or how he would overcome them, but he knew that he couldn't do it alone. He would need to rely on the forest, on the magic that flowed through it, and on the wisdom of those who had come before him.

As he stood up and prepared to leave the clearing, Finn felt a sense of determination settle over him. The road ahead was uncertain, filled with dangers and challenges that he couldn't yet imagine. But he was ready, and he would face whatever came his way with the courage and humility that the faerie had spoken of.

With one last glance at the pool, Finn turned and walked back into the forest, his footsteps sure and steady. The trees closed in around him, their branches forming a protective canopy overhead, and the whispering of the leaves filled the air, a constant reminder that the forest was watching, guiding him on his journey.

And as he ventured deeper into the woods, the faerie's words echoed in his mind, a reminder that the forest was not just a place of magic and wonder, but a place of balance and harmony, where every action had consequences, and where understanding came at a cost.

Finn knew that his journey was far from over, and that the Eternal Forest had many more secrets to reveal. But he also knew that he was not alone—the forest was with him, and he would face whatever challenges lay ahead with the strength and wisdom that the faeries had bestowed upon him.

And so, with the light of the Heart of the Forest guiding his way, Finn continued on his path, ready to uncover the mysteries of the Eternal Forest and to learn the lessons that it had to offer.

Chapter 5: The Sacred Grove

Discovering the Heart of the Forest

The Eternal Forest had a rhythm all its own, a pulse that beat in time with the heartbeat of the world itself. The deeper one ventured into its heart, the more one could feel this rhythm—an ancient, timeless cadence that resonated in the very marrow of the bones. Finn had felt this pulse since the moment he had entered the forest, a subtle hum that had grown stronger with each step he took into its depths. It was as if the forest was alive, a vast living entity that watched, listened, and breathed alongside him.

After his encounter with the faeries, Finn felt a renewed sense of purpose, but also a greater awareness of the forest's power. He had seen glimpses of its magic, had felt its presence in the whispers of the trees and the shimmering light of the faeries, but he knew that there was much more to discover. The Eternal Forest was a place of mystery, and Finn was determined to uncover its secrets, no matter where they might lead him.

The day after he met the faeries, Finn set out once more, following a narrow trail that wound through the thick underbrush. The path was faint, barely visible beneath the layers of fallen leaves and moss, but it seemed to call to him, guiding him deeper into the forest. The air was cool and crisp, the scent of pine and earth filling his lungs with each breath. Sunlight filtered through the dense canopy above, casting dappled patterns of light and shadow on the forest floor.

As he walked, Finn couldn't shake the feeling that he was being watched. It wasn't an unsettling sensation, but rather a sense of presence—an awareness that the forest was observing him, guiding him, and perhaps even testing him. The trees seemed to lean in closer, their branches swaying gently in the breeze, and the whispering of the leaves was a constant murmur in his ears.

The trail led him through a series of small clearings, each one more beautiful and serene than the last. The wildflowers were in full bloom, their vibrant colors standing out against the rich green of the grass. The sound of trickling water reached his ears, and he soon came upon a small stream that wound its way through the forest, its clear waters sparkling in the sunlight. Finn paused to drink from the stream, the cold water refreshing as it flowed over his lips.

He continued on, the trail leading him deeper into the forest, where the trees grew taller and the undergrowth thicker. The light grew dimmer, the shadows longer, and the air took on a cool, almost damp quality. The whispering of the trees grew louder, more insistent, as if they were trying to tell him something. Finn listened carefully, but the words were still indistinct, just beyond his understanding.

Then, as he rounded a bend in the trail, Finn suddenly found himself standing at the edge of a vast, open glade. He stopped in his tracks, his breath catching in his throat as he took in the sight before him.

The glade was unlike anything he had ever seen. It was enormous, easily the size of a small village, with the trees forming a perfect circle around its perimeter. The grass was a deep, rich green, so vibrant that it almost seemed to glow in the sunlight. In the center of the glade stood a single, towering tree, its trunk as wide as a house and its branches reaching high into the sky. The tree's bark was a silvery white, smooth and unblemished, and its leaves shimmered with a soft, golden light.

But it wasn't just the tree that caught Finn's attention. The entire glade seemed to pulse with energy, a tangible force that filled the air and made the hairs on the back of his neck stand on end. The light here was different too—softer, warmer, as if the very air was infused with magic. Finn could feel it in his bones, in the very core of his being. This was no ordinary glade; this was a place of power, a place of deep significance within the forest.

Finn took a hesitant step forward, his eyes fixed on the towering tree at the center of the glade. As he did so, he felt the ground beneath his feet shift, as if the very earth was alive and responding to his presence. The sensation was both exhilarating and humbling, and for a moment, Finn hesitated, unsure if he was worthy to enter such a sacred place.

But the forest seemed to beckon him forward, and Finn found himself moving toward the tree, his steps slow and reverent. As he approached, he noticed that the grass beneath his feet was softer than any he had ever walked on, as if it had been woven from the finest silk. The air was filled with the sweet scent of blooming flowers, and the soft hum of magic was a constant presence in his ears.

When he reached the base of the tree, Finn stopped and looked up, craning his neck to take in its full height. The tree was massive, its trunk rising high above him before branching out into a dense canopy that cast the entire glade in dappled shade. The leaves rustled softly in the breeze, their golden light reflecting off the smooth bark and creating a mesmerizing dance of light and shadow.

Finn reached out tentatively, his hand hovering just inches from the tree's bark. He could feel the warmth radiating from it, a gentle, comforting heat that seemed to seep into his very soul. With a deep breath, he placed his hand against the tree's trunk, and the moment he made contact, a surge of energy shot through him, powerful and overwhelming.

It was as if the tree was alive, truly alive, not just in the way that all trees are alive, but in a way that made Finn feel as though he was touching the heart of the forest itself. The energy that flowed through the tree was ancient, timeless, and filled with a wisdom that went beyond human understanding. It was a connection to something far greater than himself, something that had existed long before he was born and would continue to exist long after he was gone.

Finn closed his eyes, letting the energy wash over him, fill him, and for a moment, he felt as though he was a part of the tree, a part of the forest. He could feel the life coursing through its roots, deep in the earth, spreading out to touch every part of the forest. He could feel the warmth of the sun on its leaves, the cool touch of the breeze as it rustled through the branches. He could hear the whispers of the other trees, their voices blending together in a chorus of life and magic.

And then, as suddenly as it had begun, the connection faded, and Finn was left standing there, his hand still resting against the tree, his breath coming in shallow gasps. He felt drained, as though the experience had taken something from him, but at the same time, he felt more alive than he ever had before. The tree had shown him a glimpse of its world, its existence, and Finn knew that he had been given a rare and precious gift.

He stepped back from the tree, his heart still racing, and looked around the glade. It was then that he noticed something he hadn't seen before—other creatures were gathered around the base of the tree, their forms barely visible in the dappled light. They were of all shapes and sizes, some familiar, others completely alien, but all radiating a sense of power and grace.

There were deer with coats of shimmering silver, their antlers adorned with delicate, glowing flowers. There were wolves with fur as dark as night, their eyes burning with an inner fire. There were birds with wings of gold, their feathers catching the light and sending it scattering in a thousand different directions. And there were creatures that defied description—beings of pure energy, their forms shifting and changing as they moved, leaving trails of light in their wake.

These were the most powerful creatures of the forest, the guardians of its deepest secrets, and they had gathered here, in the Sacred Grove, to be near the Heart of the Forest. Finn felt a deep sense of awe and reverence as he watched them, knowing that he was in the presence of beings far older and wiser than himself.

As if sensing his thoughts, one of the creatures—a large, majestic stag with antlers that seemed to glow with an inner light—stepped forward, its eyes fixed on Finn. The stag moved with a grace and elegance that belied its size, its hooves barely making a sound as they touched the soft grass. When it reached Finn, it lowered its head, its antlers brushing against the ground in a gesture of respect.

Finn was momentarily taken aback by the stag's actions, unsure of how to respond. But then, without thinking, he bowed his head in return, his heart pounding in his chest. The stag raised its head, its eyes meeting Finn's, and in that moment, Finn felt a connection between them—an understanding that went beyond words. The stag seemed to be acknowledging him, recognizing him as someone who had been chosen by the forest.

The stag turned and began to walk away, its movements slow and deliberate. Finn watched as it made its way to the base of the tree, where it stood beside a large, glowing flower that had bloomed from one of the tree's roots. The flower was unlike any Finn had ever seen, its petals a deep, vibrant blue, with a golden light emanating from its center. The stag lowered its head to the flower, inhaling its scent before gently nibbling at one of its petals.

As the stag did so, a soft, golden light began to emanate from the flower, spreading out to encompass the entire glade. The light was warm and comforting, and Finn could feel it filling him with a sense of peace and tranquility. The other creatures in the glade seemed to respond to the light as well, their forms glowing with a soft, ethereal light as they moved closer to the tree.

It was as if the entire glade had come alive, the creatures and the tree working together in perfect harmony. Finn could feel the magic in the air, a powerful force that flowed through everything in the glade, connecting them all in a web of life and energy. It was a magic that went beyond anything he had ever experienced, a magic that was both ancient and timeless, a magic that was at the very heart of the forest.

For a long time, Finn simply stood there, watching the creatures as they moved around the tree, their movements slow and graceful. He felt a deep sense of peace, a sense of belonging that he had never felt before. The glade was a place of power, a place where the magic of the forest was at its strongest, and Finn knew that he had been given a rare and precious gift—to witness this sacred place, to be a part of it, even if only for a short time.

As the light began to fade, the creatures slowly began to disperse, returning to the shadows of the forest. The stag was the last to leave, its glowing antlers the final light in the glade as it disappeared into the trees. Finn watched it go, a sense of longing filling his heart as the glade returned to its natural state.

He knew that he couldn't stay in the glade forever, that his journey was far from over. The Sacred Grove had shown him a glimpse of the forest's true power, but there were still many more secrets to uncover, many more challenges to face. But as he prepared to leave the glade, Finn knew that he would carry the memory of this place with him, a reminder of the beauty and magic that lay at the heart of the forest.

With a final, reverent bow to the great tree at the center of the glade, Finn turned and began to make his way back to the trail. The forest was quiet, the only sound the soft rustling of leaves in the breeze, and Finn felt a deep sense of peace as he walked. The whispering of the trees had returned, but this time, the words were clear, their voices filled with a sense of joy and contentment.

As he left the glade behind, Finn knew that he had been changed by the experience. The Sacred Grove had shown him a world of magic and wonder, a world that existed beyond the ordinary, and Finn knew that he would never see the forest in the same way again. He had been given a rare and precious gift, a glimpse into the heart of the forest, and he knew that he would carry that memory with him for the rest of his life.

The trail led him back through the forest, the trees closing in around him as he walked. The light grew dimmer, the shadows longer, but Finn felt no fear. The Sacred Grove had filled him with a sense of peace and tranquility, a sense of belonging that he had never felt before. The forest was his home now, his place of power, and he knew that he would protect it with all his strength.

As he walked, Finn felt the pulse of the forest in his veins, the rhythm of the trees and the earth guiding his steps. He knew that his journey was far from over, that there were still many more challenges to face, but he felt ready for whatever lay ahead. The Sacred Grove had shown him the true power of the forest, and Finn knew that he would carry that power with him, a force that would guide him through the trials to come.

And so, with the memory of the Sacred Grove fresh in his mind, Finn continued on his journey, his steps sure and steady, his heart filled with the magic of the forest. The Eternal Forest was a place of mystery and wonder, a place where the ordinary and the extraordinary merged into one, and Finn knew that he was only just beginning to uncover its secrets.

As the light of the day began to fade, Finn felt a sense of anticipation build within him. The forest was alive with possibilities, and he knew that the Sacred Grove was just the beginning. There were still many more wonders to discover, many more creatures to meet, and Finn was ready for whatever lay ahead.

With a final glance back at the trail, Finn set his sights on the horizon, the light of the setting sun casting long shadows across the forest floor. The Sacred Grove had shown him the heart of the forest, but now it was time to explore its soul. The journey ahead would be long and difficult, but Finn knew that he was ready.

The forest was his guide, his teacher, and Finn was ready to learn. The Sacred Grove had opened his eyes to the true power of the Eternal Forest, and Finn knew that he would never be the same. The forest had become a part of him, just as he had become a part of the forest, and together, they would face whatever challenges lay ahead.

With a sense of purpose and determination, Finn continued on his journey, the Sacred Grove a memory that would stay with him forever. The forest was his home now, and he was ready to face whatever lay ahead.

The adventure of a lifetime awaited him, filled with wonders and dangers beyond his wildest imagination. And though he did not yet know it, Finn's journey into the heart of the Eternal Forest was only just beginning.

Chapter 6: The Cursed Lake

The Legend of the Water Spirits

The Eternal Forest was a place of endless wonder and beauty, but it was also a land where light and darkness existed in delicate balance. Finn had already witnessed the forest's splendor, from the Sacred Grove's serene magic to the playful mischief of the faeries. Yet, as he ventured deeper into the woods, he couldn't shake the feeling that he was approaching something far darker, something that contrasted sharply with the forest's otherwise harmonious existence.

For days, Finn had wandered through the dense foliage, guided by little more than instinct and the subtle whispers of the trees. The path was less clear now, overgrown with tangled vines and thick underbrush, and the air was heavy with moisture, clinging to his skin like a damp shroud. The light filtering through the canopy above was muted, casting the forest in a perpetual twilight that deepened the sense of foreboding that had settled in Finn's chest.

It was on the third day of his journey into this part of the forest that Finn first caught sight of the lake.

The forest began to thin, the towering trees giving way to shorter, scraggly ones that grew close to the ground, their roots twisting out of the earth like gnarled fingers. The air grew colder, the ground beneath his feet soggy and treacherous. The silence here was different from the peaceful stillness of the Sacred Grove—this was a silence heavy with secrets, a silence that seemed to press down on him from all sides.

And then, through the trees, Finn saw it: a vast expanse of water, dark and still, stretching out as far as the eye could see. The lake's surface was like a sheet of black glass, reflecting the overcast sky above with eerie clarity. The water was so dark that it seemed bottomless, a void that swallowed all light and gave nothing back. The air around the lake was cold, colder than it had any right to be, and it carried with it a faint, metallic tang that left a bitter taste on Finn's tongue.

Finn stood at the edge of the lake, staring out over its unnervingly calm surface. There was something about the lake that felt wrong, something that sent a shiver down his spine and made the hair on the back of his neck stand on end. He could sense the magic here, but it was different from the magic he had felt in the Sacred Grove. This was a darker, older magic, tainted by sorrow and despair.

As he stood there, the silence of the lake seemed to grow louder, the absence of sound more oppressive with each passing moment. The trees around the lake were twisted and stunted, their branches bare of leaves, and the ground was littered with the decaying remnants of plants that had long since withered and died. Even the birds and insects that had filled the forest with their songs were absent here, as if they dared not approach the water's edge.

Finn couldn't shake the feeling that he was being watched. He scanned the shore, his eyes searching for any sign of movement, but there was nothing—only the still, black water and the lifeless trees. And yet, the sensation persisted, a prickling at the back of his mind that told him he was not alone.

Slowly, cautiously, Finn took a step closer to the water. The ground beneath his feet squelched with every step, and he had to fight the urge to retreat, to turn and run back into the safety of the forest. But something held him there, a curiosity that outweighed his fear, a need to understand the dark history that hung over this place like a pall.

When he reached the water's edge, Finn knelt down, peering into the lake's depths. The water was so dark that he couldn't see more than a few inches below the surface, but he had the distinct impression that something was moving beneath the water, something that was aware of his presence.

He dipped his hand into the water, expecting it to be icy cold, but to his surprise, it was warm—warmer than the air around him. The water felt thick, almost oily, and it left a slick residue on his skin when he pulled his hand back. Finn wiped his hand on his cloak, his unease growing with each passing moment.

And then, as he stared into the water, he saw them.

At first, it was just a faint movement, a ripple that disturbed the surface of the lake. But then the water began to churn, small waves lapping against the shore as something rose from the depths. Finn watched, his breath catching in his throat, as a figure emerged from the water.

It was a woman—or at least, it had the shape of a woman. Her skin was as pale as the moon, almost translucent, and her long, dark hair clung to her body, wet and heavy. She was beautiful, in a haunting, otherworldly way, but there was something about her that filled Finn with dread. Her eyes were dark, empty voids, and her expression was one of profound sorrow.

The woman hovered just above the surface of the water, her feet not quite touching the lake. She stared at Finn with those empty eyes, and Finn felt as though she was looking through him, seeing not just his physical form, but his very soul.

"Who are you?" Finn asked, his voice trembling despite his efforts to keep it steady.

The woman didn't respond. She simply stared at him, her expression unchanged, her eyes unblinking. Then, slowly, she raised one hand and pointed to the lake, her movements slow and deliberate.

Finn followed her gaze, his eyes drifting back to the water. The surface of the lake had gone still once more, but there was something beneath it, something that glowed with a faint, ethereal light. It was a pale, ghostly glow, barely visible in the dark water, but it was there—a light that seemed to pulse with a life of its own.

Finn stared at the light, entranced by its faint glow, but then he noticed something else. The light wasn't alone. All around it, more lights began to appear, each one faint and distant, but unmistakable. They hovered just below the surface, moving slowly and deliberately, like will-o'-the-wisps in the night.

It took Finn a moment to realize what he was seeing. These were not just lights—they were spirits, trapped beneath the surface of the lake, their faint glow the only sign of their presence.

Finn felt a wave of sorrow wash over him as he stared at the spirits, their movements slow and listless. He could feel their despair, their longing for freedom, and it tore at his heart. These spirits were not here by choice—they were trapped, bound to the lake by some ancient curse.

He turned back to the woman, his voice barely above a whisper. "What happened to you?"

The woman's expression didn't change, but there was a flicker of something in her eyes—pain, sorrow, a deep and abiding sadness that seemed to weigh down on her like a physical burden. She lowered her hand, her gaze drifting back to the lake, and Finn knew that she would not, or could not, answer him.

But then, from somewhere deep within the forest, he heard a voice—a soft, melodious voice that seemed to drift on the breeze, carried by the wind to his ears.

"Once, long ago, this lake was a place of beauty and light, a place where the water spirits danced beneath the moonlight, their laughter echoing through the trees. They were the guardians of the lake, its protectors and keepers, and they lived in harmony with the creatures of the forest."

The voice was gentle, soothing, and it filled Finn with a sense of calm, despite the dark history it spoke of. He turned his head, searching for the source of the voice, but there was no one there—only the forest, the lake, and the pale woman who hovered above the water.

"But the spirits' happiness was not to last," the voice continued, a note of sorrow creeping into its tone. "For a great darkness came upon the land, a darkness that sought to claim the lake and its magic for itself. The spirits fought bravely, but they were no match for the darkness. One by one, they fell, their bodies sinking into the depths of the lake, their souls bound to its waters by the curse of the darkness."

Finn felt a lump form in his throat as the voice spoke. He could picture it in his mind—the spirits, once joyful and free, now trapped beneath the surface of the lake, their laughter silenced, their light dimmed.

"And so they remain," the voice said, its tone heavy with regret. "Bound to the lake for all eternity, cursed to dwell in its depths, unable to find peace or rest. They are the Cursed Lake's tragic guardians, their souls forever intertwined with the waters that claimed them."

Finn swallowed hard, his heart aching for the spirits and the woman who stood before him. He wanted to help them, to free them from their curse, but he didn't know how. The magic that held them was ancient and powerful, far beyond anything he had ever encountered.

The woman's gaze shifted back to Finn, her empty eyes filled with a silent plea. Finn could feel the weight of her sorrow, the desperation in her gaze, and it nearly broke him. He wanted to reach out, to touch her, to offer her some small comfort, but he knew that he couldn't—not while she was bound to the lake.

"What can I do?" Finn asked, his voice hoarse with emotion. "How can I help you?"

For a long moment, the woman didn't respond. Then, slowly, she raised her hand once more and pointed to the far side of the lake, where the trees grew tall and thick, their branches forming a dense canopy that blocked out the light.

"There," she said, her voice barely audible, like the rustling of leaves in the wind. "The source of the curse lies there."

Finn followed her gaze, his eyes narrowing as he peered into the darkness. The trees were so thick that he could barely make out anything beyond their tangled branches, but he could sense it—a presence, a dark and malevolent force that seemed to pulse with a life of its own.

He turned back to the woman, determination hardening in his chest. "I'll find it," he said, his voice steady. "I'll find the source of the curse and destroy it. I'll free you."

The woman's eyes flickered with something like hope, and she nodded slowly, her hand falling back to her side. "Be careful," she whispered, her voice so faint that Finn had to strain to hear it. "The darkness is strong... and it does not let go easily."

Finn nodded, his resolve firm. He didn't know what awaited him on the far side of the lake, but he knew that he couldn't turn back now. These spirits had been cursed for centuries, trapped in the lake's depths, their lives stolen from them by a force beyond their control. He couldn't leave them to their fate—not when there was a chance, however slim, that he could help them.

With one last look at the woman, Finn turned and began to make his way around the shore of the lake. The ground was treacherous, the mud sucking at his boots with every step, and the cold air bit at his skin, but he pressed on, driven by a sense of purpose that burned within him.

As he walked, he kept his eyes on the trees that loomed ahead, their dark silhouettes stark against the grey sky. The presence he had felt earlier was growing stronger, more oppressive, and he could feel it pressing down on him, as if the very air was thick with malevolence.

The further he walked, the more the forest around him seemed to change. The trees were twisted and gnarled, their branches bare of leaves, and the ground was littered with the decaying remnants of plants that had long since withered and died. Even the air seemed different—thicker, colder, filled with a sense of dread that gnawed at Finn's resolve.

But he didn't stop. He couldn't stop. The woman's sorrowful gaze was burned into his mind, a constant reminder of what was at stake. These spirits had been trapped for centuries, their lives stolen from them by a force beyond their control. He couldn't leave them to their fate—not when there was a chance, however slim, that he could help them.

Finally, after what felt like hours of walking, Finn reached the far side of the lake. The trees here were taller, their branches forming a dense canopy that blocked out what little light remained. The ground was covered in thick moss, slick and treacherous, and the air was cold, colder than anywhere else in the forest.

And there, nestled between the trees, was a cave.

The entrance to the cave was narrow, barely wide enough for Finn to squeeze through, and the darkness inside was absolute, impenetrable. But there was no mistaking it—this was the source of the curse, the place where the darkness had taken root.

Finn took a deep breath, steeling himself for what lay ahead. The woman's warning echoed in his mind—the darkness was strong, and it did not let go easily. But Finn knew that he had no choice. If he wanted to free the spirits, if he wanted to break the curse, he would have to face whatever waited for him in that cave.

He took a step forward, then another, his heart pounding in his chest as he approached the entrance. The air was thick with the stench of decay, and the darkness seemed to press in on him from all sides, but he didn't waver. He had come too far to turn back now.

When he reached the entrance, Finn paused, his hand resting on the cold, slick stone of the cave's mouth. The darkness within seemed to pulse with a life of its own, a malevolent force that seemed to beckon him deeper, and Finn felt a shiver run down his spine.

But he didn't let the fear take hold. With one final, steadying breath, Finn stepped into the darkness.

The cave was cold, colder than anything Finn had ever experienced. The air was so frigid that it hurt to breathe, and his breath came out in frosty plumes that hung in the air like ghosts. The walls of the cave were slick with moisture, and the ground was uneven, covered in loose stones that threatened to trip him with every step.

But Finn pressed on, his steps slow and cautious as he made his way deeper into the cave. The darkness was absolute, a void that swallowed everything it touched, and Finn had to feel his way along the walls, his hands brushing against the cold, damp stone.

As he descended further into the cave, the air grew thicker, the stench of decay stronger, and Finn could feel the presence of the darkness growing more oppressive, pressing down on him from all sides. It was as if the cave itself was alive, a living entity that sought to consume him, to drag him down into its depths and never let him go.

But Finn didn't stop. He couldn't stop. The spirits were counting on him, and he had to see this through, no matter what.

After what felt like an eternity, the tunnel began to widen, and Finn found himself standing in a large, open chamber. The air here was even colder, the stench of decay nearly overpowering, and the darkness was so thick that it seemed to pulse with a life of its own.

And there, in the center of the chamber, was the source of the curse.

It was a stone altar, ancient and weathered, its surface covered in strange, twisted runes that glowed with a faint, sickly light. The air around the altar was thick with malevolent energy, a darkness so deep and so powerful that it seemed to pull at the very fabric of reality, warping it in ways that made Finn's head spin.

And standing before the altar was a figure, a figure cloaked in shadows, its form indistinct and constantly shifting. It was as if the darkness itself had taken shape, a malevolent force given physical form.

The figure turned to face Finn, and for a moment, Finn thought he saw a pair of glowing eyes staring out at him from the shadows. But then the darkness shifted, and the eyes were gone, leaving only the vague outline of the figure.

"Who are you?" Finn demanded, his voice echoing in the chamber. "What are you?"

The figure didn't respond. It simply stood there, its form shifting and writhing, as if it was made of smoke and shadows.

Finn took a step forward, his hand going to the hilt of his dagger. "I've come to break the curse," he said, his voice steady despite the fear gnawing at him. "I've come to free the spirits."

At his words, the figure let out a low, rumbling laugh, a sound that seemed to vibrate through the very stone of the cave. "You think you can break the curse?" it said, its voice a dark, mocking whisper. "You think you can stand against me?"

Finn tightened his grip on his dagger, his heart pounding in his chest. "I don't care what you are," he said, his voice filled with resolve. "I'm going to end this."

The figure's laughter grew louder, more menacing, and the darkness around it seemed to swell, filling the chamber with a malevolent energy that made Finn's skin crawl. "Foolish mortal," it hissed. "You cannot defeat me. I am the darkness that lies at the heart of the world, the shadow that consumes all light. I am eternal, and I will not be undone by the likes of you."

But Finn didn't back down. He could feel the spirits watching him, their sorrowful gazes urging him on, and he knew that he couldn't let them down. He had to end this, no matter the cost.

With a shout, Finn charged at the figure, his dagger held high. The figure didn't move, didn't even flinch, as Finn closed the distance between them. But just as he was about to strike, the darkness surged forward, wrapping around Finn like a shroud and dragging him to the ground.

Finn struggled, thrashing against the darkness, but it was like trying to fight against smoke. The darkness was everywhere, suffocating him, pulling him down into its depths. He could feel its cold fingers wrapping around his throat, squeezing the life out of him, and his vision began to blur.

But just as Finn thought he was lost, he heard a voice—a voice so soft that it was barely more than a whisper, but a voice that filled him with a renewed sense of hope.

"Finn..."

The voice was familiar, comforting, and it cut through the darkness like a blade. Finn's eyes snapped open, and he saw a faint light shining in the distance, a light that grew brighter with each passing moment.

"Finn... you must fight..."

The light was growing stronger, driving back the darkness, and Finn could feel its warmth filling him with strength. He didn't know where the voice was coming from, but he knew that it was right—he couldn't give up, not now.

With a surge of strength, Finn forced himself to his feet, the darkness retreating in the face of the light. The figure let out a hiss of rage, the shadows around it writhing and twisting, but Finn didn't let it intimidate him. He knew that this was his only chance.

He raised his dagger, the blade glowing with the light that had filled the chamber, and with a shout, he drove it into the altar.

The reaction was immediate. The altar shuddered, the runes on its surface glowing brighter and brighter until they were nearly blinding. The figure let out a scream, a sound that was filled with rage and despair, and the darkness around it seemed to implode, collapsing in on itself as the light consumed it.

The chamber was filled with a blinding light, and for a moment, Finn thought he had been swallowed by it. But then, as the light began to fade, he realized that he was still standing, still alive.

The altar was gone, the figure was gone, and the darkness that had filled the chamber had been banished. The air was clear, the stench of decay gone, and Finn could feel the curse lifting, the malevolent energy that had filled the lake dissipating.

He fell to his knees, his breath coming in ragged gasps, and for a long moment, he simply sat there, trying to process what had just happened. The spirits were free—the curse had been broken, and the darkness had been defeated.

Finn didn't know how long he sat there, but eventually, he felt a warmth spread through his body, a warmth that filled him with a sense of peace and contentment. He looked up, and to his surprise, he saw the woman from the lake standing before him, her pale form glowing with a soft, ethereal light.

"Thank you," she said, her voice filled with gratitude. "You have freed us."

Finn struggled to his feet, his body still trembling from the effort. "It's over," he said, his voice hoarse. "The curse is broken."

The woman nodded, a gentle smile on her lips. "Yes, thanks to you. We are free."

Finn could feel the tears welling up in his eyes, a mixture of relief and exhaustion washing over him. "I'm glad I could help," he said, his voice thick with emotion.

The woman reached out, her hand brushing against Finn's cheek, and he felt a warmth spread through him, filling him with a sense of peace. "You have a kind heart, Finn," she said softly. "The forest is lucky to have you."

Finn felt a blush rise to his cheeks, but before he could respond, the woman began to fade, her form dissolving into the light. "Farewell, Finn," she said, her voice growing fainter. "May the forest guide you on your journey."

And with that, she was gone, leaving Finn alone in the chamber.

For a long moment, Finn simply stood there, his mind reeling from everything that had just happened. The curse was broken, the spirits were free, and the darkness had been defeated. But he knew that his journey was far from over—the forest still held many secrets, many challenges that he would have to face.

But as he made his way out of the cave and back into the forest, Finn felt a renewed sense of purpose. The spirits were free, and the Cursed Lake was no longer a place of darkness and despair. It was a place of light, a place where the spirits could finally find peace.

And as he continued on his journey, Finn knew that he would carry the memory of the Cursed Lake with him, a reminder of the power of the forest and the strength of the spirits that dwelled within it.

The Eternal Forest was a place of wonder and magic, a place where the light and darkness existed in delicate balance. And Finn knew that he was only just beginning to uncover its secrets.

The adventure of a lifetime awaited him, filled with wonders and dangers beyond his wildest imagination. And though he did not yet know it, Finn's journey into the heart of the Eternal Forest was only just beginning.

Chapter 7: The Phoenix's Rebirth

Witnessing a Miracle

The Eternal Forest was a place of perpetual mystery, where each step revealed something new, something wondrous and, at times, something deeply unsettling. Finn had seen much in his time wandering these ancient woods—beauty beyond compare, darkness that chilled the soul, and magic so potent it defied explanation. Yet, despite all he had encountered, there was a persistent feeling that he had only begun to scratch the surface of the forest's many secrets.

As he continued his journey, the memory of the Cursed Lake lingered in his mind. The spirits he had freed weighed heavily on his thoughts, their sorrow a reminder of the deep and sometimes tragic history that the forest held. But the Eternal Forest was also a place of balance, where life and death, sorrow and joy, existed in a delicate equilibrium. It was this balance that intrigued Finn the most, and it was this balance that he sought to understand.

After the events at the Cursed Lake, Finn found himself drawn to the heart of the forest once more, guided by a sense of purpose that he couldn't quite explain. The trees here were different—taller, older, their branches reaching higher into the sky, as if trying to touch the heavens. The air was warmer, carrying with it the faint scent of pine and something else, something he couldn't quite place. It was a scent that was both familiar and foreign, comforting yet mysterious.

The path beneath his feet was well-trodden, but it felt ancient, as if countless beings had walked it before him. The forest around him was alive with sound—the chirping of birds, the rustle of leaves in the wind, and the distant, melodic song of a stream. Yet, there was an underlying tension in the air, a sense of anticipation that made Finn's heart beat a little faster.

He followed the path deeper into the forest, his footsteps light and careful. The trees grew closer together here, their trunks thick and gnarled, their roots weaving in and out of the earth like the veins of some great, living being. The canopy above was dense, allowing only slivers of sunlight to filter through, casting the forest floor in a dappled, golden light.

As he walked, Finn began to notice a change in the air. It was growing warmer, almost uncomfortably so, and the scent he had noticed earlier was becoming stronger, more intense. It was a smell of smoke and something else, something sweet and intoxicating, like the scent of flowers in full bloom.

The warmth in the air grew more intense, and Finn could feel it on his skin, a dry heat that reminded him of the few times he had ventured into the deserts far beyond the forest's borders. The path beneath his feet became softer, the earth warm and dry, and the trees took on a different appearance. Their bark was darker, their leaves thicker and more vibrant, with shades of red, orange, and gold that seemed to shimmer in the sunlight.

Finn's steps slowed as he took in his surroundings. He had never seen this part of the forest before—it was as if he had crossed some invisible threshold into a place where the rules of the natural world didn't quite apply. The air was thick with magic, a potent, almost tangible force that seemed to pulse with every beat of his heart.

And then, through the trees, he saw it.

At first, it was just a flicker of light, a flash of color that stood out against the dark trunks of the trees. But as Finn drew closer, the light grew brighter, more intense, until it was almost blinding. He shielded his eyes with one hand, squinting against the glare, but he couldn't look away.

The source of the light was a tree, but not like any tree Finn had ever seen. It was enormous, its trunk wide and twisted, its branches reaching high into the sky like the fingers of a giant. The bark of the tree was a deep, rich red, and its leaves were a brilliant gold, glowing with an inner light that seemed to pulse in time with the beat of Finn's heart.

But it wasn't just the tree that caught Finn's attention—it was what was nestled among its branches. High up, near the top of the tree, was a nest, and in that nest was a creature of such beauty and power that it took Finn's breath away.

It was a bird, but not just any bird. Its feathers were a brilliant red, orange, and gold, shimmering like flames in the sunlight. Its wings were wide and powerful, each feather perfectly formed and glowing with an inner light. Its eyes were a deep, piercing blue, filled with intelligence and wisdom, and its beak and talons were sharp and strong, gleaming like polished metal.

This was no ordinary bird—this was a Phoenix.

Finn had heard of the Phoenix before, of course—who hadn't? It was a creature of legend, a bird of fire and renewal, said to be immortal, constantly reborn from its own ashes. The Phoenix was a symbol of hope, of rebirth, and of the endless cycle of life and death. But to see one with his own eyes, to witness the beauty and majesty of such a creature, was something Finn had never imagined.

The Phoenix sat in its nest, its wings folded gracefully at its sides, its head held high as it surveyed the forest below. There was a regal air about it, a sense of power and authority that radiated from its very being. And yet, there was also a softness to its gaze, a warmth that seemed to reach out and touch Finn's very soul.

For a long moment, Finn simply stood there, staring up at the Phoenix in awe. The heat in the air was intense, but it didn't burn—instead, it was a comforting warmth, like the heat of a fire on a cold winter's night. The scent of smoke and flowers filled his lungs, and the light of the Phoenix bathed the entire area in a golden glow.

And then, as if sensing Finn's presence, the Phoenix turned its head and looked directly at him. Its piercing blue eyes met Finn's, and in that moment, Finn felt as though the Phoenix was looking deep into his soul, seeing not just his physical form, but everything that he was—his thoughts, his hopes, his fears.

The connection was brief, but powerful. Finn felt a wave of emotions wash over him—wonder, awe, and something else, something deeper and more profound. It was as if the Phoenix was communicating with him, speaking to him in a language that went beyond words.

And then, just as quickly as it had begun, the connection was broken. The Phoenix turned its gaze away, looking back out over the forest, and Finn was left standing there, his heart pounding in his chest.

For a moment, he wasn't sure what to do. The Phoenix was a creature of legend, a being of immense power and significance, and Finn felt unworthy to even be in its presence. But something urged him forward, a sense of purpose that he couldn't ignore.

Slowly, carefully, Finn began to approach the tree. The heat grew more intense with each step, and the light of the Phoenix seemed to grow brighter, but Finn pressed on. He could feel the magic in the air, a powerful force that seemed to hum with life, and it drew him forward, compelling him to continue.

When he reached the base of the tree, Finn stopped and looked up. The Phoenix was still perched in its nest, its wings folded at its sides, its gaze fixed on something far beyond the forest. The tree's trunk was warm to the touch, and the air around it shimmered with heat, distorting the light and creating the illusion of flames dancing in the air.

Finn placed a hand on the trunk of the tree, feeling the warmth seep into his skin. The bark was smooth, almost silky, and it seemed to pulse with a life of its own. The magic here was different from anything Finn had encountered before—it was ancient, powerful, and filled with a sense of renewal and rebirth.

He looked up at the Phoenix once more, and as he did, he noticed something strange. The bird's feathers, once so vibrant and full of life, were beginning to change. They were losing their luster, the brilliant colors fading to a dull, ashen gray. The Phoenix's wings drooped slightly, and its head lowered, as if the weight of the world had suddenly become too much to bear.

Finn's heart ached at the sight. He had heard stories of the Phoenix's cycle of death and rebirth, how it would build a nest of fragrant wood, set it ablaze, and be consumed by the flames, only to rise from its own ashes, renewed and reborn. But to witness it firsthand, to see the great bird in its final moments, was something entirely different.

The Phoenix let out a soft, mournful cry, a sound filled with sorrow and resignation. It was a sound that spoke of endings, of the inevitable passage of time, and of the pain that came with letting go. The sound resonated deep within Finn, filling him with a profound sense of loss.

And yet, there was also a sense of hope—a sense that this was not the end, but rather a new beginning. The Phoenix was a creature of fire and renewal, a symbol of the endless cycle of life and death, and Finn knew that its death was not a true ending, but a necessary part of the cycle.

As the Phoenix's feathers continued to fade, the light around it grew dimmer, the warmth in the air becoming less intense. The bird let out another cry, this one softer, more plaintive, and Finn could feel the magic in the air shifting, changing, as if the very fabric of reality was being altered.

Finn watched in silence as the Phoenix began to lower itself into its nest. The once-vibrant feathers were now completely gray, and the bird's movements were slow, almost sluggish, as if it was using the last of its strength to prepare for what was to come.

The nest itself was made of branches and twigs, but there was something unusual about it. The branches were intertwined with leaves and flowers that glowed with a faint, ethereal light, and the entire structure seemed to radiate a gentle warmth. It was a nest fit for a creature as magnificent as the Phoenix, a place of rest and renewal.

The Phoenix settled into the nest, its head resting on its chest, its wings folded around its body. For a long moment, it remained still, its eyes closed, as if gathering its strength for the final act. The air around the tree was heavy with anticipation, the magic in the air thick and potent.

And then, with a sudden, intense burst of light, the Phoenix erupted into flames.

The fire was unlike any Finn had ever seen—bright and fierce, but with a beauty that took his breath away. The flames danced and swirled around the Phoenix, their colors shifting from red to orange to gold, and the heat was so intense that Finn had to take a step back, shielding his eyes from the brilliance.

But despite the intensity of the flames, there was no fear, no pain. The Phoenix's cry was one of release, of acceptance, and the fire that consumed it was not one of destruction, but of transformation. The flames were a cleansing force, burning away the old to make way for the new, and Finn could feel the power of the rebirth in the very air around him.

The fire blazed for what felt like an eternity, the heat radiating out in waves, filling the forest with its warmth. The light of the flames reflected off the trees, casting long shadows that danced and flickered in the golden glow. And through it all, Finn stood in awe, his heart filled with a mixture of sorrow and hope, as he witnessed the miracle of the Phoenix's rebirth.

Finally, as the flames began to die down, the light in the air faded, and the heat lessened. The fire that had consumed the Phoenix was now little more than a smoldering ember, and the once-magnificent bird was gone, reduced to a pile of ash that lay in the center of the nest.

Finn felt a lump form in his throat as he stared at the ashes. The Phoenix, a creature of legend and power, was gone. But even as he mourned the loss, he knew that this was not the end. The Phoenix was a symbol of renewal, of hope, and Finn knew that it would rise again.

The air around the tree was still warm, the scent of smoke and flowers lingering in the breeze. The forest was quiet, as if holding its breath, waiting for what was to come. Finn took a step closer to the tree, his eyes fixed on the ashes in the nest.

And then, as if in response to his thoughts, the ashes began to stir.

At first, it was just a faint movement, a gentle shifting of the gray powder. But then, as Finn watched, the ashes began to glow with a soft, golden light, the same light that had filled the air before the Phoenix's death. The glow grew brighter, more intense, until it was almost blinding, and the ashes began to rise, swirling and coalescing in the air above the nest.

Finn's breath caught in his throat as he watched the miracle unfold. The ashes, once the remnants of a life that had ended, were now transforming, reshaping themselves into something new, something magnificent. The light grew brighter, the warmth more intense, and Finn could feel the magic in the air reaching its peak, a powerful force that seemed to resonate with the very core of his being.

And then, with a sudden burst of light, the Phoenix was reborn.

The bird emerged from the ashes, its wings spread wide, its feathers glowing with a brilliant, fiery light. The colors were even more vibrant than before—deep reds, oranges, and golds that shimmered and flickered like flames. The Phoenix's eyes, once dull and lifeless, were now a piercing blue, filled with a renewed sense of life and purpose.

The Phoenix let out a powerful cry, a sound that echoed through the forest, filled with strength and determination. It was a cry of triumph, of victory over death, and it resonated deep within Finn, filling him with a sense of hope and renewal.

The bird's wings beat powerfully, sending gusts of warm air through the forest as it took to the sky. The flames that had surrounded it were now gone, replaced by a radiant light that seemed to shine from within. The Phoenix soared above the trees, its movements graceful and fluid, and Finn could feel the power of its rebirth in every beat of its wings.

For a long time, Finn watched the Phoenix as it flew above the forest, its brilliant light illuminating the trees below. It circled the tree that had been its home, its nest, and then, with one final, powerful cry, it flew off into the distance, disappearing into the horizon.

Finn stood there, his heart pounding in his chest, his mind reeling from everything he had just witnessed. The Phoenix's rebirth was more than just a spectacle—it was a powerful symbol of hope, of renewal, of the endless cycle of life and death. It was a reminder that even in the darkest of times, there was always the possibility of a new beginning, a fresh start.

The warmth in the air began to fade, the light growing dimmer as the Phoenix's presence receded. The forest around Finn was quiet, peaceful, as if it too had been touched by the magic of the Phoenix's rebirth. The scent of smoke and flowers still lingered, a faint reminder of the miracle that had just occurred.

Finn took a deep breath, his mind still processing everything he had seen. The Phoenix was gone, but its presence lingered in the air, a sense of renewal and hope that filled him with a newfound sense of purpose. The Eternal Forest was a place of wonder, of beauty, of magic, and Finn knew that he had been given a rare and precious gift—to witness the rebirth of the Phoenix, to be a part of the endless cycle of life and death that defined this ancient place.

As he turned to leave the clearing, Finn felt a sense of peace settle over him, a calm that he hadn't felt since he first entered the forest. The journey ahead was still uncertain, still filled with challenges and dangers, but he felt ready, more ready than he had ever been.

The Phoenix's rebirth had shown him that no matter how dark the world might seem, there was always the possibility of a new beginning, of hope rising from the ashes. It was a lesson that Finn knew he would carry with him for the rest of his life, a lesson that would guide him on his journey through the Eternal Forest and beyond.

With one last look at the tree, now standing silent and still, Finn turned and made his way back into the forest. The path ahead was long, and there were still many more secrets to uncover, many more wonders to witness. But Finn felt ready—ready to face whatever lay ahead, ready to continue his journey through this magical, ancient forest.

The light of the Phoenix had faded, but its warmth remained, a beacon of hope that would guide Finn on his journey. The Eternal Forest was a place of miracles, a place where the impossible became reality, and Finn knew that he was only just beginning to uncover its secrets.

As he walked, the forest around him seemed to come alive once more—the birds began to sing, the leaves rustled in the breeze, and the sound of the stream's gentle song filled the air. The world was filled with life, with beauty, with magic, and Finn felt a deep sense of gratitude for the gift he had been given.

The Phoenix's rebirth was a miracle, a powerful symbol of hope and renewal, and Finn knew that it was a reminder of the endless cycle of life and death that defined the Eternal Forest. It was a lesson that he would carry with him always, a reminder that even in the darkest of times, there was always the possibility of a new beginning, a fresh start.

And so, with a heart filled with hope and determination, Finn continued on his journey, ready to face whatever lay ahead, knowing that the Eternal Forest was a place of endless wonder and that the adventure of a lifetime was still to come.

Chapter 8: The Shadow of the Serpent

Facing the Forest's Darkest Threat

The Eternal Forest was known for its beauty, its magic, and its profound mysteries. But Finn had always sensed that, beneath its wondrous surface, there lay something darker, something dangerous and unsettling. The forest thrived on balance—light and shadow, life and death, creation and destruction. This balance had guided him through the many wonders of the forest, from the Sacred Grove to the Phoenix's Rebirth, but now, as Finn ventured deeper into the heart of the forest, he began to feel the weight of its darker side pressing in on him.

The air was thick, heavy with moisture and the scent of decay. The forest floor was soft beneath Finn's boots, his steps sinking slightly into the moss-covered earth with each footfall. The trees around him were ancient, their bark gnarled and twisted, their branches hanging low as if weighed down by the centuries of time they had endured. The deeper Finn walked, the more oppressive the atmosphere became. The light filtering through the canopy above had dimmed to a faint, sickly green, and the usual sounds of the forest—birds, insects, and the rustling of leaves in the wind—had all but vanished.

Finn knew something was wrong. He had felt the change gradually, as if the forest itself was holding its breath, waiting for something to happen. It wasn't just the absence of sound or the thickening air that unnerved him—it was the feeling of being watched. That same sense of unseen eyes following his every move had grown stronger over the past few hours, and now it was almost unbearable. The forest, once his guide and companion, now felt like a living entity that was judging him, testing him.

He tightened his grip on the hilt of his dagger, the familiar weight of the blade comforting him in the face of the unknown. Though Finn had encountered many creatures in the Eternal Forest—some benevolent, others mischievous—he had always felt some level of control, some sense that he was in harmony with the forest. But here, in this dark and ancient part of the woods, the rules felt different. The balance he had come to rely on seemed fragile, as though it could shatter at any moment.

The path he was following—if it could even be called a path—had long since faded into the thick underbrush. The trees grew closer together here, their trunks gnarled and twisted like the limbs of some ancient, forgotten beast. Vines hung low, dripping with moisture, and the air was thick with the smell of damp earth and rotting wood. Every step felt like a challenge, as though the forest itself was trying to prevent Finn from moving forward.

And yet, something pulled him onward.

There was a darkness ahead, deeper than the shadows cast by the trees, a darkness that seemed to pulse with its own malevolent energy. Finn could feel it like a weight on his chest, growing heavier with each step he took. The forest was alive with it—this oppressive, creeping darkness that seemed to suffuse everything around him.

After what felt like hours of walking, Finn finally reached a clearing. But it was unlike any clearing he had seen before. The ground here was bare, devoid of the lush grass and wildflowers that usually covered the forest floor. Instead, the earth was cracked and dry, the color of old bones. The trees that bordered the clearing were twisted and blackened, their bark charred as if by some ancient fire. Even the air here felt different—thicker, heavier, with a metallic tang that clung to the back of Finn's throat.

In the center of the clearing, a massive stone altar stood, its surface covered in strange, serpentine carvings. The stone was smooth and cold, its dark surface reflecting no light. Finn approached cautiously, his instincts telling him that this place was important, that it held some dark secret.

But before he could get too close, he felt it.

A presence.

It was subtle at first, a low hum at the edge of his senses, like the faint vibration of the earth beneath his feet. But then it grew stronger, more tangible, until it felt like a cold hand pressing against his chest, making it hard to breathe. Finn stopped in his tracks, his heart pounding in his ears as the sensation grew overwhelming.

And then, he saw it.

At the far edge of the clearing, slithering out from the shadows of the blackened trees, was a creature so massive and so terrifying that it took Finn's breath away. It was a serpent—easily thirty feet long, its body as thick as a tree trunk and covered in scales that glistened in the dim light like polished obsidian. Its eyes were slits of molten gold, and its tongue flicked out of its mouth, tasting the air as it moved silently across the ground.

The Serpent.

Finn had heard stories of this creature, whispered in taverns and around campfires. It was said to be as old as the forest itself, a being of pure malevolence and cunning, capable of twisting the minds of those who crossed its path. Some said it was a guardian of the forest's darkest secrets, while others claimed it was a force of chaos, bent on destroying the balance that held the Eternal Forest together.

Whatever the truth, Finn knew one thing for certain: the Serpent was a threat. A threat to him, to the forest, and to everything he had come to care about.

The Serpent moved with terrifying grace, its massive body coiling and uncoiling as it slithered toward the altar. It didn't seem to notice Finn at first, or perhaps it simply didn't care. Its golden eyes were fixed on the stone altar, and as it reached the base of the structure, it began to coil its body around the stone, its scales rasping against the surface with a sound that made Finn's skin crawl.

For a moment, Finn considered running. Every instinct in his body screamed at him to turn and flee, to get as far away from the Serpent as possible. But something held him in place—a sense of duty, perhaps, or the knowledge that if he ran now, the Serpent would continue to threaten the forest, unchecked.

Finn's hand tightened around the hilt of his dagger, but he knew that a single blade would be useless against a creature of this size. The Serpent was massive, ancient, and far more powerful than anything he had ever faced. If he was going to stop it, he would need more than just steel.

The Serpent's head rose above the altar, its golden eyes gleaming with a cold, predatory intelligence. Finn could feel the weight of its gaze, the oppressive pressure that seemed to fill the air around him. The creature's tongue flicked out once more, tasting the air, and then—slowly—it turned its gaze toward Finn.

Time seemed to slow as their eyes met. Finn felt a chill run down his spine, a cold, creeping dread that seemed to settle deep in his bones. The Serpent's gaze was unlike anything he had ever experienced—it was ancient, powerful, and filled with a malevolence that seemed to seep into his very soul.

For a long moment, neither of them moved. The Serpent remained coiled around the altar, its head raised, its eyes fixed on Finn. And then, slowly, it began to speak.

"I have been watching you."

The voice was a low hiss, like the rustling of dry leaves in the wind. It filled the clearing, seeming to come from all around Finn, echoing in his mind as much as his ears.

"I have seen your journey, traveler. I have felt your presence in my forest."

Finn swallowed hard, his throat dry. The Serpent's words sent a chill through him, but he forced himself to remain calm, to keep his voice steady.

"This isn't your forest," Finn said, his voice hoarse. "The forest belongs to all its creatures—not just to you."

The Serpent's eyes narrowed, and for a moment, Finn thought he had made a terrible mistake. The creature's body shifted, its coils tightening around the altar, and the ground beneath Finn's feet seemed to tremble.

"You think you understand this place, boy?" the Serpent hissed, its voice filled with contempt. "You think you know the Eternal Forest, its secrets, its power?"

Finn's heart pounded in his chest, but he refused to back down. He knew that showing fear would only make the Serpent stronger, and if there was one thing he had learned in his time in the forest, it was that the creatures here—no matter how powerful—could be reasoned with.

"I don't claim to understand everything," Finn said, his voice steady despite the fear gnawing at him. "But I know enough to see that you're a threat to the balance of this place. The forest can't survive if darkness like yours is allowed to spread."

The Serpent let out a low, rumbling laugh, a sound that made Finn's skin crawl. Its massive body shifted, and it began to uncoil from the altar, its head lowering until it was level with Finn's. The creature's golden eyes gleamed with a predatory light, and Finn could see the sharp, curved fangs glistening in its mouth.

"Balance," the Serpent hissed, the word dripping with disdain. "You speak of balance as if you understand it. But the truth is, there can be no balance without me. I am the shadow, the darkness that gives meaning to the light. Without me, this forest would wither and die."

Finn shook his head, his grip tightening on his dagger. "You're wrong," he said, his voice firm. "The forest doesn't need you—it thrives on harmony, on the balance between creation and destruction, life and death. But you... you only bring chaos."

The Serpent's eyes flashed with anger, and for a moment, Finn thought it might strike. But instead, the creature's body tensed, and it let out another low, hissing laugh.

"You are a fool, traveler," the Serpent said, its voice cold and mocking. "You think you can stop me? You think you can fight the darkness that I represent?"

Finn swallowed hard, his heart pounding in his chest. The Serpent's words were like a weight pressing down on him, and for a moment, he felt a flicker of doubt. The creature was ancient, powerful, and cunning—far beyond anything he had ever faced. How could he hope to defeat something like this?

But then, Finn remembered the lessons he had learned during his time in the forest. The Phoenix's rebirth had shown him that even in the darkest of times, there was always the possibility of renewal, of hope. The Sacred Grove had taught him the importance of balance, of harmony between light and dark. And the spirits of the Cursed Lake had shown him that even the most ancient of curses could be broken.

He couldn't let fear control him—not now.

"I won't let you destroy this forest," Finn said, his voice steady and filled with resolve. "I won't let you tip the balance."

The Serpent's eyes narrowed, and its body tensed, coiling in on itself as if preparing to strike. Finn knew that the time for words was over—the Serpent wasn't going to let him leave without a fight.

Finn took a deep breath, his heart pounding in his chest. He knew that he couldn't defeat the Serpent with brute strength alone—this was a creature of cunning and darkness, a creature that thrived on fear and manipulation. If he was going to survive this, he would need to outsmart it.

The Serpent struck, its massive body lunging forward with terrifying speed. Finn barely had time to react, diving to the side just as the creature's jaws snapped shut where he had been standing moments before. The ground shook as the Serpent's body collided with the earth, and Finn rolled to his feet, his dagger drawn.

The Serpent's head whipped around, its golden eyes gleaming with fury. It struck again, faster this time, but Finn was ready. He ducked beneath the creature's jaws, slashing out with his dagger as he moved. The blade glanced off the Serpent's scales, barely leaving a scratch, but Finn didn't let that deter him.

The Serpent let out a furious hiss, its body coiling and uncoiling as it prepared for another strike. Finn could see the muscles rippling beneath its scales, the raw power that it possessed, but he knew that if he could keep his wits about him, he might be able to find a weakness.

The Serpent lunged once more, and this time, Finn didn't dodge. Instead, he stood his ground, waiting until the last possible moment before throwing himself to the side. The creature's jaws snapped shut inches from his face, and Finn drove his dagger into the soft flesh beneath its jaw.

The Serpent let out a deafening roar of pain, its body writhing in agony as Finn wrenched his dagger free. The creature's blood, dark and viscous, dripped from the blade, and Finn took a step back, his breath coming in ragged gasps.

But the Serpent wasn't done. With a furious hiss, it reared back, its body coiling tightly as it prepared for one final, devastating strike.

Finn's mind raced. He knew that he couldn't survive another attack like that. The Serpent was too powerful, too fast. But then, his eyes fell on the stone altar behind the creature, and an idea began to form in his mind.

The Serpent lunged, its massive body hurtling toward Finn with terrifying speed. But this time, Finn was ready. Instead of dodging to the side, he ran forward, ducking beneath the creature's jaws and sprinting toward the altar.

The Serpent's head whipped around, its eyes blazing with fury, but it was too late. Finn reached the altar and leapt onto its surface, his dagger raised high.

The Serpent reared back, its body coiling tightly as it prepared for one final, devastating strike. Finn could feel the air around him growing thick with malevolent energy, the weight of the Serpent's power pressing down on him. But he didn't hesitate.

With a shout, Finn drove his dagger into the center of the altar, piercing the stone with a loud crack. The ground beneath him trembled, and the air was suddenly filled with a deafening roar as the Serpent's body convulsed, its massive coils thrashing wildly.

Finn jumped back from the altar, his heart pounding in his chest as he watched the Serpent writhe in agony. The creature's eyes, once filled with cold, predatory intelligence, were now wide with fear, and its body began to disintegrate, dissolving into shadow and smoke.

The Serpent let out one final, ear-splitting roar, and then—just as suddenly as it had appeared—it was gone.

The clearing was silent once more, the oppressive weight of the Serpent's presence lifted. The air felt lighter, clearer, and Finn could feel the balance of the forest returning, the darkness receding.

He stood there for a long moment, his breath coming in ragged gasps, his body trembling from the effort. The Serpent was gone, defeated, but the weight of the battle still lingered in the air.

Finn wiped the sweat from his brow, his mind reeling from everything that had just happened. The Serpent had been a creature of pure malevolence, a force of darkness that threatened the very balance of the Eternal Forest. But Finn had faced it, had stood his ground, and had survived.

The forest around him seemed to come alive once more—the birds began to sing, the leaves rustled in the breeze, and the air was filled with the scent of fresh earth and blooming flowers. The balance had been restored, and the Eternal Forest was at peace once more.

Finn sheathed his dagger, his heart filled with a mixture of relief and exhaustion. The battle was over, but he knew that his journey was far from complete. The Eternal Forest still held many secrets, many challenges that he would have to face.

But for now, Finn allowed himself a moment of peace, a moment to breathe, to reflect on everything that had happened. The Serpent, the darkness, the battle—it was all part of the forest's delicate balance, a balance that Finn had come to understand and respect.

With one last look at the stone altar, now cracked and weathered, Finn turned and made his way back into the forest. The path ahead was long, and there were still many more wonders to uncover, many more challenges to face.

But Finn felt ready.

The Serpent had been a formidable foe, a creature of darkness and chaos. But Finn had faced it, had stood his ground, and had emerged victorious. The Eternal Forest was a place of beauty, of magic, of mystery—and Finn knew that he was only just beginning to uncover its secrets.

With a heart filled with hope and determination, Finn continued on his journey, ready to face whatever lay ahead, knowing that the Eternal Forest was a place of endless wonder and that the adventure of a lifetime was still to come.

Chapter 9: The Hidden Village

Discovering the Forest's Human Inhabitants

The Eternal Forest had always been a place of untold mysteries and astonishing magic, but after his harrowing encounter with the Serpent, Finn found himself yearning for a brief respite. The battle with the Serpent had drained him, both physically and mentally, and while he had triumphed in preserving the forest's balance, he now sought something less dangerous, something that could remind him of the peace and beauty he had initially found in the forest.

For days, Finn wandered deeper into the woods, following paths that were little more than faint trails beneath the towering trees. The air around him had grown lighter since his victory over the Serpent, the oppressive darkness having receded, but there was still a quiet tension in the forest, as if it was waiting for something. He had come to trust the rhythm of the forest, the whispers of the leaves, and the occasional guidance of the creatures he encountered, yet this time, it felt as though the forest was leading him somewhere deliberate, as if beckoning him toward something he had not yet seen.

The trees here were different, too. Tall and ancient, with trunks so thick that it would take several men to encircle one, their bark smooth and pale like polished stone. Sunlight filtered down through the canopy in thin, golden shafts, illuminating patches of wildflowers and moss-covered rocks. The air was warmer, carrying with it the faint scent of pine and fresh earth, and the usual sounds of the forest—birds singing, the rustling of leaves in the wind, and the occasional snap of a twig—filled the air with a sense of life and movement.

It was on the third day of this aimless wandering that Finn noticed something unusual. As he walked through a particularly dense part of the forest, he came upon a small, winding stream. The water was clear and cool, babbling gently as it wound its way over smooth stones and fallen branches. But what caught Finn's attention wasn't the stream itself—it was the small wooden bridge that spanned it.

The bridge was simple, made of roughly hewn logs lashed together with vines, yet it was clearly man-made. This was the first sign of human presence Finn had encountered in the forest, and it stopped him in his tracks. For all the magic and mystery of the Eternal Forest, he had never considered the possibility that people might live here, hidden away from the outside world.

Intrigued, Finn crossed the bridge, his boots thudding softly against the wooden planks. On the other side of the stream, the forest began to change. The trees were still tall and ancient, but there was a sense of order to them now, as if they had been deliberately planted in neat rows. The underbrush had thinned, and the ground was covered in a soft, thick carpet of moss, making his steps nearly silent.

As he walked, Finn began to notice other signs of human activity—small, hand-carved totems placed at the base of trees, woven baskets filled with herbs and flowers, and the faint scent of woodsmoke on the breeze. The further he went, the stronger the feeling became that he was not alone, and yet, there was no sense of danger here. If anything, the atmosphere was one of tranquility, of a deep, abiding peace that seemed to permeate the very air.

After what felt like an hour of walking, Finn came upon a clearing, and what he saw took his breath away.

Nestled in the heart of the clearing was a village—small, humble, and yet so perfectly integrated into the landscape that it was almost as if it had grown from the forest itself. The houses were built of wood and stone, their roofs thatched with straw and covered in moss, making them blend seamlessly with the trees that surrounded them. Each house was positioned beneath the shade of a towering oak or pine, their windows facing the clearing where a communal fire pit stood at the center.

The villagers themselves moved about with a quiet grace, their clothing simple but elegant, made of natural fibers dyed in the soft, muted colors of the forest. They carried baskets of fruit, herbs, and flowers, and tended to small gardens filled with vegetables and medicinal plants. Children played near the stream, their laughter filling the air, while elders sat on wooden benches, weaving baskets or carving intricate designs into wooden staves.

Finn stood at the edge of the clearing, watching in awe as the village went about its daily life. It was unlike anything he had ever seen—a community of people living in perfect harmony with the forest, their lives so deeply intertwined with the natural world that it was impossible to tell where the village ended and the forest began.

As he watched, a young woman noticed him standing at the edge of the clearing. She had long, dark hair that flowed down her back in loose waves, and her skin was tanned from years spent working in the sun. She wore a simple dress made of woven cloth, dyed a soft shade of green, and around her neck hung a necklace of small, polished stones. She smiled warmly at Finn, her dark eyes twinkling with curiosity.

"Hello," she called out, her voice soft and melodic. "You're a traveler, aren't you?"

Finn nodded, stepping forward into the clearing. "Yes, I am. I didn't mean to intrude—I didn't know there were people living this deep in the forest."

The young woman's smile widened, and she gestured for Finn to follow her. "You're not intruding. We don't get many visitors here, but you're welcome to stay for as long as you like. Come, I'll take you to the elder. She'll want to meet you."

Finn hesitated for a moment, but the woman's warm, open demeanor put him at ease. He followed her through the village, taking in the sights and sounds around him. The people here moved with a quiet, deliberate grace, their movements unhurried, as though time itself flowed differently in this hidden place. There was a deep sense of community, of shared purpose, that Finn hadn't encountered in any other village he had visited.

As they walked, the young woman introduced herself. "My name is Mira," she said, glancing back at Finn with a smile. "What's yours?"

"Finn," he replied. "How long has your village been here?"

Mira's expression grew thoughtful. "No one really knows. The village has been here for as long as anyone can remember. We've lived in the forest for generations, always in harmony with the land and the creatures that call it home. It's the only life we've ever known."

Finn nodded, his curiosity piqued. "And the forest? How do you live so closely with its magic?"

Mira's smile returned. "The forest is our home, and we've learned to respect its rhythms, its cycles. The forest provides everything we need—food, shelter, medicine—and in return, we protect it, care for it. The creatures of the forest are our allies, our friends. They help us, and we help them."

As she spoke, Finn began to understand just how deeply connected these people were to the forest. They weren't just living off the land—they were part of it, woven into the fabric of the forest's magic in a way that few outsiders could ever hope to comprehend. It was a way of life that was both simple and profound, a life lived in perfect balance with the natural world.

They reached the largest house in the village, a structure made of smooth stone and wood, with a roof covered in thick moss and vines. Mira led Finn inside, where the air was cool and filled with the scent of herbs and burning incense.

Sitting near the hearth was an elderly woman, her long white hair braided down her back. She wore a robe made of finely woven cloth, dyed a deep shade of forest green, and around her neck hung a pendant carved from a single piece of polished wood. Her eyes, though clouded with age, were sharp and piercing, filled with the wisdom of many years.

Mira approached the elder with a respectful bow. "Elder Liora, this is Finn. He's a traveler, and he's come from outside the forest."

The elder's gaze shifted to Finn, her eyes narrowing slightly as she studied him. For a moment, she said nothing, her expression unreadable. Then, slowly, a smile crept across her face.

"Welcome, traveler," she said, her voice soft but strong. "It's been many years since we've had a visitor from the outside world. Please, sit with me. I'd like to hear your story."

Finn hesitated for a moment, then nodded and sat down across from the elder. He wasn't sure where to begin—how could he explain everything he had experienced in the Eternal Forest? The wonders he had seen, the dangers he had faced, the lessons he had learned?

But as he looked into the elder's wise, patient eyes, he felt a sense of calm wash over him. He began to speak, telling her about his journey through the forest, the creatures he had encountered, and the magic that had guided him along the way. He told her about the Sacred Grove, the Phoenix's rebirth, and his battle with the Serpent.

As he spoke, Elder Liora listened in silence, her expression thoughtful. When Finn finished, she nodded slowly, her eyes filled with understanding.

"You've seen much of the forest's magic," she said softly. "And you've learned much. But there is still more for you to discover."

Finn nodded, his curiosity growing. "What more is there? What haven't I seen?"

Elder Liora's gaze drifted to the window, where the sunlight filtered through the trees outside. "The Eternal Forest is a place of balance," she said. "A place where light and shadow, life

and death, exist in harmony. But there are forces at work in the forest that seek to disrupt that balance. The Serpent you fought was one such force, but it is not the only one."

Finn felt a chill run down his spine. "What do you mean?"

The elder's gaze returned to Finn, her expression grave. "The forest is ancient, older than any of us can comprehend. And with that age comes power—power that can be both a blessing and a curse. There are creatures in the forest that seek to harness that power for their own purposes, creatures that would upset the balance and bring chaos to the land."

Finn's heart pounded in his chest. He had known, of course, that the forest was a place of great magic and mystery, but he hadn't realized just how precarious its balance truly was.

"The village," Elder Liora continued, "exists to protect the forest. For generations, we have lived in harmony with the land and its creatures, ensuring that the balance is maintained. But we cannot do it alone. The forest has chosen you, Finn, to help us in this task."

Finn's mind raced. The forest had chosen him? It was a daunting thought, but it also filled him with a sense of purpose. He had come to the Eternal Forest seeking adventure, seeking answers to the mysteries of the world, but now it seemed that the forest had other plans for him.

"What do I need to do?" Finn asked, his voice steady despite the weight of the task before him.

Elder Liora smiled, a glimmer of warmth returning to her eyes. "For now, rest. You've been through much, and there is still more to come. But when the time is right, the forest will guide you."

Finn nodded, his mind still racing with questions. But he knew that the elder was right—he needed to rest, to gather his strength for whatever challenges lay ahead.

As he stood to leave, Mira approached him with a smile. "Come," she said. "I'll show you to a place where you can rest."

Finn followed her out of the elder's house and back into the village. The sun was beginning to set, casting the clearing in a warm, golden light. The villagers were finishing their tasks for the day, and the air was filled with the soft hum of quiet conversation and the crackling of the communal fire.

Mira led Finn to a small, cozy house at the edge of the clearing, nestled beneath the shade of a massive oak tree. The house was simple, but comfortable, with a bed covered in soft furs and a small table adorned with a bowl of fresh fruit and a jug of water.

"You can stay here for as long as you like," Mira said, her smile warm. "The village is a safe place, and you'll always be welcome here."

Finn nodded, feeling a sense of gratitude wash over him. "Thank you," he said softly. "This village... it's unlike anything I've ever seen. It's so peaceful, so connected to the forest."

Mira's smile widened. "It's our home," she said simply. "We've lived here for generations, and we've learned that the forest provides everything we need. It's a life of balance, of harmony with the land and its creatures."

Finn couldn't help but admire the village and its people. They had created a way of life that was in perfect harmony with the natural world, a life free from the chaos and destruction that so often plagued the outside world.

As the sun dipped below the horizon, casting the village in a soft, golden glow, Finn felt a deep sense of peace settle over him. The village was a sanctuary, a place of calm and tranquility in the midst of the wild and unpredictable forest. And for the first time since he had entered the Eternal Forest, Finn felt truly at home.

That night, as he lay beneath the soft furs of his bed, listening to the gentle rustling of leaves outside his window, Finn's mind drifted to the task ahead. The forest had chosen him, and though he didn't yet know what that meant or what challenges lay ahead, he felt a deep sense of purpose.

The Eternal Forest was a place of balance, of light and shadow, life and death. And it was his task to help preserve that balance, to protect the magic of the forest from those who sought to destroy it.

With that thought in mind, Finn closed his eyes and drifted off to sleep, his dreams filled with the sound of the forest's gentle whispers and the promise of the journey that still lay ahead.

Chapter 10: The Legend of the Eternal Flame

Unraveling the Forest's Greatest Secret

The Eternal Forest was filled with ancient myths and legendary creatures, but among all the stories whispered beneath the trees, none was as elusive, nor as powerful, as the tale of the Eternal Flame. Finn had heard only fragments of the legend during his travels, but each mention was enough to ignite a fire of curiosity in his heart. The village had given him peace, and the wisdom of Elder Liora had guided him, but there was something deeper in the forest—something older, more dangerous, and more alluring than anything he had yet encountered.

The village elders spoke of the Eternal Flame with reverence, their eyes flickering with fear and awe whenever its name was mentioned. It was said to be the heart of the forest, a fire that burned eternally, granting unimaginable power to those who found it. But the Flame was not to be sought lightly; its seekers had to prove themselves worthy, for the trials guarding the Eternal Flame were perilous. Many had tried, but none had ever returned.

Finn had spent days in the village, recovering from his journey and learning about the ways of the forest people. Their connection to the land was deep, their respect for its balance unwavering. But even here, among the most knowledgeable guardians of the forest, the Eternal Flame remained shrouded in mystery.

One evening, as the sun set over the trees and the sky blazed with the hues of twilight, Finn sat with Elder Liora near the village's central fire. The embers glowed warmly, casting flickering shadows on the ground, and the scent of burning pine filled the air. Finn had been hesitant to ask about the Flame, knowing how guarded the village was about its secrets, but his curiosity had grown too strong to ignore.

"Elder Liora," he began cautiously, watching her as she stirred the fire with a long stick. "I've heard whispers of something called the Eternal Flame. Some say it's a myth, others that it's real. What do you know of it?"

Liora's hands stilled, and for a long moment, she said nothing. The silence stretched between them, heavy with unspoken words. Finally, she lifted her gaze to Finn, her eyes reflecting the glow of the fire, and sighed.

"The Eternal Flame," she said slowly, her voice carrying the weight of centuries. "It is not a myth, though many wish it were. It is real, and its power is beyond anything you can imagine."

Finn leaned forward, his heart quickening. "What is it exactly? And why do people seek it?"

Liora shifted her gaze back to the fire, her expression distant as if recalling something from long ago. "The Flame is ancient, older than the forest itself. Some say it was born from the stars, a fragment of the universe that fell to the earth and ignited a fire that has never died. Others believe it is the embodiment of life itself, the purest form of magic in existence. Whatever its origin, the Eternal Flame has become a symbol of ultimate power, capable of granting great wisdom, strength, and even immortality to those who are deemed worthy."

She paused, her hands tightening on the stick she held. "But the Flame is also dangerous. Its power is too great for most to wield, and the trials one must face to reach it are unforgiving. Those who seek the Flame must prove themselves in every way—physically, mentally, and spiritually. And even then, the Flame may choose to consume them instead of granting its gifts."

Finn felt a chill run down his spine. "Has anyone ever found it?"

Liora shook her head, a look of sorrow passing over her face. "Many have tried. Some of our own people have sought the Flame, believing they were strong enough to face the trials. None have returned."

Finn's mind raced as he absorbed her words. The Eternal Flame was real. Its power was real. And the dangers that surrounded it were just as real. But the more he learned, the more he felt drawn to it. The Flame was the greatest secret of the forest, the key to understanding its deepest magic. If he could find it, if he could survive its trials, he might finally unravel the mysteries of the Eternal Forest.

"I want to find it," Finn said, his voice quiet but determined.

Liora looked at him sharply, her expression grave. "No, Finn. You don't understand what you're saying. The Flame is not something to be sought lightly. The forest itself will turn against you if you try. It is a test like no other—a test of your very soul."

Finn met her gaze, his heart steady despite the fear gnawing at him. "I understand the risks. But if the Flame is the heart of the forest, if it holds the key to its balance, then I have to try. The Serpent was only one threat—there may be others, and the Flame could be the only way to protect the forest."

For a long time, Liora said nothing, her eyes searching Finn's face as if weighing his resolve. Finally, she sighed and nodded, her shoulders sagging with the weight of her decision.

"If you are truly determined," she said, her voice heavy with resignation, "then I will tell you what I know. But be warned, Finn—the path to the Eternal Flame is one that has claimed many lives. You must be prepared to face your darkest fears, your deepest weaknesses, and to confront the very essence of who you are."

Finn nodded, his resolve hardening. "I'm ready."

Liora studied him for a moment longer before rising to her feet. She gestured for Finn to follow her, and together, they walked away from the fire and into the shadows of the forest. The trees closed in around them, their branches swaying gently in the breeze, and the soft glow of the village fire faded behind them.

As they walked, Liora spoke in hushed tones, her voice barely audible over the rustling leaves. "The Eternal Flame is hidden deep within the forest, in a place few have ever seen. It is said to burn in a temple built long ago by the ancients, a place where time itself is distorted, and reality bends to the will of the Flame."

She paused, her eyes flicking to Finn's. "The path to the temple is treacherous. It is guarded by trials—trials that will test every part of you. The forest will become your adversary, twisting your surroundings, distorting your sense of time and space. You will face illusions, creatures of darkness, and perhaps even your own mind turned against you."

Finn's breath quickened, but he forced himself to remain calm. He had faced danger before. He had fought the Serpent, freed the spirits of the Cursed Lake, and witnessed the rebirth of the Phoenix. Whatever trials awaited him on the path to the Flame, he would face them head-on.

Liora stopped at the base of a towering oak tree, its trunk wide and gnarled, its roots spreading out like the fingers of a giant hand. She turned to face Finn, her expression solemn.

"This is where the path begins," she said softly, gesturing to the tree. "Beyond this point, you are on your own. No one can guide you through the trials—you must rely on your own strength, your own instincts. The Flame will test you, Finn, and it will not be kind."

Finn nodded, his heart pounding in his chest. "Thank you, Elder Liora. For everything."

Liora's gaze softened, and for a moment, she reached out and placed a hand on Finn's shoulder. "May the forest guide you, Finn. And may you find the strength to face whatever lies ahead."

With that, she turned and walked back toward the village, leaving Finn alone at the edge of the path. The air around him was still, the forest silent as if holding its breath. Finn took a deep breath, steeling himself for what was to come, and stepped forward.

The path wound its way through the forest, growing narrower and more overgrown with each step. The trees pressed in on either side, their branches hanging low and casting long shadows across the ground. The air grew colder, the scent of pine and earth replaced by something darker, more ominous. Finn could feel the magic in the air thickening, a palpable force that seemed to press against his skin, and with every step he took, the sense of being watched grew stronger.

The first trial came sooner than Finn expected.

As he rounded a bend in the path, he found himself standing at the edge of a wide, yawning chasm. The ground beneath his feet crumbled away into darkness, and across the gap, barely visible in the dim light, was the continuation of the path. A narrow stone bridge spanned the chasm, but it was old, weathered, and looked as though it could collapse at any moment.

Finn stepped cautiously to the edge of the chasm, peering down into the abyss. He couldn't see the bottom—only darkness, stretching endlessly below him. The air was thick with the scent of damp earth, and the sound of wind whistling through the chasm sent a shiver down his spine.

He knew this was the first test. The forest was already playing with his senses, trying to unnerve him, to make him doubt his own abilities. The bridge looked fragile, but there was no other way forward. He would have to trust in himself—and in the forest—to get across.

Taking a deep breath, Finn stepped onto the bridge. The stones shifted beneath his weight, and for a moment, he thought the entire structure would collapse, sending him plummeting into the darkness below. But the bridge held, and Finn took another step, his heart pounding in his chest.

The further he walked, the more unstable the bridge became. The stones cracked and shifted beneath his feet, and the wind whipped around him, making it difficult to keep his balance. But Finn kept moving, his eyes fixed on the far side of the chasm, refusing to look down.

Halfway across, the ground beneath him gave way.

With a cry, Finn fell, his arms flailing as he tried to catch himself. His fingers scraped against the rough stone, and for a terrifying moment, he dangled over the edge of the bridge, his feet kicking against the empty air.

His heart raced, his breath coming in ragged gasps. The darkness below seemed to reach up for him, threatening to pull him down into its depths. But Finn gritted his teeth, his fingers tightening their grip on the stone, and with a surge of strength, he pulled himself back onto the bridge.

Panting, he crouched there for a moment, his hands trembling. The forest was testing him, pushing him to his limits. But he wasn't going to let it break him. He had come too far to turn back now.

With renewed determination, Finn rose to his feet and continued across the bridge. The rest of the journey was just as treacherous, but he kept his focus, his movements steady and deliberate. Finally, after what felt like an eternity, he reached the far side of the chasm and stepped onto solid ground.

His legs felt weak, his breath shallow, but he had made it. The first trial was over.

The path ahead twisted and turned, leading deeper into the forest. The air grew colder, the trees taller and more gnarled, their branches twisting together like the bones of long-dead giants. The light dimmed, and soon, Finn found himself walking in near darkness, the only sound the soft crunch of leaves beneath his boots.

The second trial came in the form of an illusion.

As Finn walked, the trees around him began to shift. The shadows lengthened, twisting and warping until they no longer resembled trees at all. The air grew thick with mist, and strange shapes moved within it—figures, barely visible, flitting through the fog like ghosts.

Finn's heart pounded in his chest as the figures drew closer, their forms becoming more defined. They were people—familiar people. His family, his friends, people he had known long ago. They reached out to him, their voices soft and pleading.

"Finn," they whispered. "Come back. Come back to us."

Finn shook his head, trying to clear the fog from his mind. This wasn't real. He knew it wasn't real. But the figures were so lifelike, so familiar, that for a moment, he hesitated. What if they were real? What if the forest had somehow brought them here?

"Finn," the voices called again, their hands reaching for him. "Don't leave us."

His mother's face appeared in the mist, her eyes filled with tears. "Finn, please."

The sight of her nearly broke him. She had died years ago, taken by an illness that had swept through their village. He had been there at her bedside, holding her hand as she took her last breath. And now, here she was, standing before him, alive and whole.

"Mom?" Finn's voice cracked, his heart aching with the longing to believe it was real.

But deep down, he knew it wasn't. This was the forest's magic at work, an illusion designed to test him, to make him doubt his own reality.

With a deep breath, Finn closed his eyes, willing the illusion to fade. "You're not real," he whispered, his voice shaking. "This isn't real."

When he opened his eyes again, the figures were gone. The mist had lifted, and the forest had returned to its normal state. The path lay before him, winding its way deeper into the trees.

Finn took a shaky breath, his heart still pounding in his chest. The illusion had been more powerful than he had expected, but he had seen through it. He had passed the second trial.

As he continued on the path, Finn felt the weight of the forest's magic pressing down on him, heavier with each step. The trials were becoming more intense, more personal, and he knew that the hardest part was yet to come.

The final trial awaited him at the temple.

The path led him to a clearing, and there, at the center, stood a structure unlike anything Finn had ever seen. The temple was massive, its walls made of smooth black stone that gleamed in the dim light. The architecture was ancient, its design both beautiful and imposing, with intricate carvings of serpents and flames adorning the walls.

At the top of a long flight of stone steps stood the entrance to the temple, two massive doors made of polished metal. And beyond those doors, Finn knew, was the Eternal Flame.

He had come this far. He had faced the forest's trials, and now, only one final challenge remained.

Taking a deep breath, Finn climbed the steps and pushed open the doors.

The chamber beyond was vast, its walls lined with torches that flickered with an eerie, unnatural light. At the center of the chamber, on a raised platform, burned the Eternal Flame.

It was unlike any fire Finn had ever seen. The flames were a deep, vibrant blue, and they danced and swirled in a way that seemed almost alive. The heat radiating from the Flame was intense, but it was not the kind of heat that burned—it was a warmth that seemed to seep into Finn's very soul, filling him with a sense of power and awe.

But as Finn stepped closer to the Flame, he felt a presence—a dark, oppressive force that seemed to rise from the very ground beneath his feet.

The Flame was watching him.

And now, the final trial began.

Finn could feel the weight of the Flame's gaze pressing down on him, testing him, searching for any weakness. This was not a trial of physical strength or even mental fortitude. This was a trial of the soul.

The Flame would see everything—his hopes, his fears, his desires, his failures. It would see his deepest flaws, the darkness within him that he had tried so hard to hide. And if it found him unworthy, it would consume him.

Finn stood before the Flame, his heart pounding in his chest. He had come this far, but now, at the very end, he wasn't sure if he was ready. Could he face the truth about himself? Could he confront the darkness within and still prove himself worthy?

The Flame flared, its light growing brighter, and Finn felt its power surge through him, filling every part of his being.

And in that moment, Finn understood.

The Flame was not something to be conquered, nor was it something to be feared. It was a reflection of the forest itself—beautiful, powerful, and dangerous. It was a force of creation and destruction, life and death, balance and chaos. And to face it, to truly understand it, Finn had to embrace all of those things within himself.

With a deep breath, Finn opened himself to the Flame.

The heat washed over him, and for a moment, he felt as though he was burning, consumed by the Flame's power. But then, just as quickly, the sensation faded, replaced by a deep sense of peace.

The Flame had accepted him.

The chamber was silent, the only sound the soft crackling of the Flame. Finn stood there for a long time, staring into its depths, his mind still reeling from the experience.

He had found the Eternal Flame. He had faced its trials, and he had been deemed worthy.

But as Finn turned to leave the temple, he realized something important: the Flame's power was not his to wield. It was not a tool, not a weapon. It was a force of nature, something that existed beyond human understanding. And while he had been granted the knowledge he sought, the Flame had also taught him a valuable lesson.

The power of the Eternal Flame lay not in its ability to grant strength or immortality, but in its ability to remind him of the delicate balance of the forest. The Flame was the heart of the forest, a symbol of the eternal cycle of life and death, creation and destruction. And Finn, like all who had come before him, was just a part of that cycle.

As he left the temple and stepped back into the forest, Finn felt a deep sense of gratitude. The journey had been difficult, the trials harrowing, but in the end, he had found what he was truly searching for: an understanding of the forest, of its magic, and of his place within it.

The Eternal Forest was a place of balance, of light and shadow, and the Eternal Flame was the embodiment of that balance.

And now, Finn knew that his journey was far from over.

There were still more secrets to uncover, more challenges to face. But whatever lay ahead, Finn felt ready. The Flame had shown him the truth, and now, he would carry that truth with him on the next steps of his journey through the Eternal Forest.

Chapter 11: The Trial of the Elements

Proving Worth to the Forest's Spirits

The Eternal Forest was vast and unyielding, a realm of ancient magic where the delicate balance between light and shadow was preserved by the spirits who inhabited it. These spirits, the unseen guardians of the forest, held immense power, and they watched over the land with an intensity that few outsiders ever realized. Finn had come to understand that the forest was more than just a collection of trees, creatures, and mystical places—it was a living entity, one that required respect and harmony to thrive.

After his encounter with the Eternal Flame, Finn knew that his journey through the forest was far from over. The Flame had revealed many truths, but it had also left him with a greater understanding of the challenges that lay ahead. The forest was not simply a place to be explored or conquered; it was a world of elemental forces, of ancient spirits that demanded recognition and reverence. And now, in order to truly prove his worth, Finn would have to face the Trial of the Elements.

He had heard whispers of the trial from the villagers, stories passed down through generations about those who had undergone the sacred rite. It was said that the trial tested every aspect of a person—body, mind, and soul—by challenging them with the raw, untamed power of the elements. Earth, air, fire, and water: these were the building blocks of life itself, and to pass the trial, one had to prove their mastery over all four.

Finn had no illusions about the difficulty of the task before him. The Eternal Forest had already tested him in ways he had never imagined, but this trial would be different. It wasn't just about survival or endurance; it was about showing the forest spirits that he was worthy of their favor, that he understood the balance they worked so hard to maintain.

The first step was finding the place where the trial would begin.

The villagers had spoken of an ancient glade, hidden deep within the forest, where the elements converged. It was a sacred place, one that only revealed itself to those the forest deemed worthy. Finn had no map, no clear path to follow—only his instincts and the subtle guidance of the forest itself.

For days, he wandered through the dense woods, his senses attuned to the shifting energies around him. The trees whispered to him, their leaves rustling in the wind, and the ground beneath his feet seemed to pulse with life. It was as if the forest was alive, guiding him toward the glade, testing his resolve with each step.

Finally, after what felt like an eternity of searching, Finn found himself standing at the edge of a clearing unlike any he had ever seen. The trees here were taller, their trunks twisted and gnarled, their roots sinking deep into the earth. The air was thick with the scent of damp moss and rich soil, and the sky above was a brilliant shade of blue, unmarred by clouds.

At the center of the clearing stood a large stone altar, its surface etched with ancient symbols that glowed faintly in the sunlight. Around the altar, four distinct areas were marked out, each representing one of the elements. To the north, a towering stone pillar rose from the ground, its surface rough and covered in vines—this was the domain of earth. To the east, a swirling vortex of wind spun in the air, its currents invisible but palpable—this was the domain of air. To the south, a large pyre of flames crackled and roared, their heat radiating outward in waves—this was the domain of fire. And to the west, a shimmering pool of water lay still and silent, its surface reflecting the sky above—this was the domain of water.

Finn approached the altar cautiously, his heart pounding in his chest. This was it—the Trial of the Elements. The air around him buzzed with energy, the power of the elements pressing down on him from all sides. He could feel their presence, their raw, untamed force waiting to be tested. The spirits of the forest were watching him, and the trial was about to begin.

A soft whisper carried on the wind, and though there were no visible figures, Finn knew the spirits were speaking to him, urging him forward.

"To pass the trial, you must prove yourself to each of the four elements," the voice said, as if it came from the trees themselves. "Only those who understand the balance between them can claim the favor of the forest."

Finn took a deep breath, his mind racing with anticipation and fear. He had faced many challenges in the forest, but this would be unlike anything he had encountered before. Each element would test him in its own way, and he would need to adapt, to understand the unique power and nature of each.

He walked toward the northern pillar, where the element of earth awaited him. The stone was cold and rough beneath his hand as he placed his palm against it. The ground beneath his feet trembled slightly, and the trees seemed to lean closer, as if the forest itself was holding its breath.

The trial had begun.

The Trial of Earth

The air around Finn grew still, and the sounds of the forest faded into silence. As he stood before the stone pillar, he felt a deep rumbling beneath his feet, as if the very ground was shifting and awakening. The earth was alive, and it was calling to him.

Suddenly, the ground in front of him split open, and a massive wall of stone and earth rose from the ground, blocking his path. The wall was jagged and uneven, its surface covered in thick vines and roots that twisted and writhed like living creatures. It was clear that this was his first challenge—the element of earth was testing his strength, his ability to overcome obstacles both physical and mental.

Finn stepped forward, examining the wall. It was too high to climb, and the vines that covered its surface were thick and unyielding. He would need to find another way through. The forest spirits were watching, waiting to see how he would approach the challenge.

He knelt down, placing his hand on the ground, feeling the cool earth beneath his fingers. The answer, he realized, wasn't in brute force—it was in understanding the nature of the element itself. Earth was strong, immovable, but it was also alive. It could be shaped, molded, if one knew how to work with it rather than against it.

Closing his eyes, Finn focused on the connection between himself and the earth beneath him. He could feel the energy flowing through the ground, the slow, steady pulse of life that ran through the roots of the trees, the stones, and the soil. He focused on that energy, willing it to move, to shift, to clear a path.

At first, nothing happened. But then, slowly, he felt the ground beneath him begin to tremble. The vines on the wall loosened, their grip weakening, and the stones began to shift. A narrow opening appeared at the base of the wall, just large enough for him to crawl through.

Finn smiled, his heart racing with excitement. He had passed the first part of the trial. The element of earth had tested his patience, his understanding of the natural world, and he had succeeded by working with the earth, not against it.

He crawled through the opening and emerged on the other side, where the next element awaited him.

The Trial of Air

The moment Finn stepped into the eastern section of the clearing, he felt the wind pick up around him. It swirled and danced through the trees, tugging at his hair and clothes, as if welcoming him into its domain. But there was a sharpness to the wind, a sense of danger that made him wary.

The air was alive with movement, and as Finn walked further into the clearing, the wind intensified. It whipped around him, pulling at his arms and legs, making it difficult to move forward. The sky above darkened, and the wind began to howl, a deafening roar that drowned out all other sounds.

This was the trial of air—a test of agility, of flexibility, and of understanding the invisible forces that shaped the world. Finn knew that he couldn't fight the wind; it was too powerful, too unpredictable. Instead, he would have to adapt, to move with it, to become one with the air itself.

He closed his eyes, allowing himself to feel the currents of wind that swirled around him. It was chaotic, ever-changing, but there was a rhythm to it, a pattern hidden within the turbulence. If he could find that rhythm, he could use it to his advantage.

Taking a deep breath, Finn began to move. He stepped lightly, shifting his weight with the wind's currents, allowing the gusts to carry him forward rather than push him back. The wind was strong, but Finn remained calm, adjusting his movements with each new burst of air. It was like a dance, a fluid, ever-changing motion that required complete focus and awareness.

At first, it was difficult—each gust of wind threatened to knock him off balance, to throw him to the ground. But as he continued, Finn began to understand the flow of the wind. He anticipated its movements, shifting his body to match its direction. His steps became lighter, his movements more graceful, and soon, he was moving through the wind with ease.

The wind howled around him, but Finn remained steady. He had passed the trial of air, proving his ability to adapt, to remain flexible in the face of chaos.

As the wind began to die down, Finn smiled to himself. The second trial was over, but there were still two more elements to face.

The Trial of Fire

The heat hit Finn like a wave as he approached the southern section of the clearing. Flames roared in the distance, their crackling echoing through the trees, and the air was thick with the scent of burning wood. This was the domain of fire, the most destructive and unpredictable of the elements.

Fire was a force of creation and destruction, of warmth and devastation. It was the element that both gave life and took it away, and Finn knew that this trial would be the most dangerous yet. He would have to prove his control over fire, his ability to wield its power without being consumed by it.

As he stepped closer to the roaring flames, Finn felt the heat intensify. The fire danced before him, wild and untamed, its flames licking at the sky. It was a living thing, a force of nature that cared nothing for those who stood in its path.

For a moment, Finn hesitated. How could he possibly control something so powerful, so dangerous? But then, he remembered what the Eternal Flame had taught him—the balance between creation and destruction, the delicate dance of life and death that fire embodied. He didn't need to control the fire—he needed to understand it.

Closing his eyes, Finn focused on the heat around him, on the way the flames moved and shifted. He could feel the power of the fire, the raw energy that radiated from it, but he also sensed its vulnerability. Fire needed fuel to survive, and without it, the flames would die. It was both strong and fragile, a paradox that Finn had to accept if he was to pass the trial.

Taking a deep breath, Finn stepped into the flames.

The heat was overwhelming at first, but Finn remained calm, focusing on the rhythm of the fire, on the way it consumed and grew. He moved through the flames with purpose, his steps measured and deliberate. The fire roared around him, but it did not burn him. Instead, it seemed to part before him, as if recognizing his understanding of its nature.

With each step, the flames grew smaller, their intensity waning. The fire no longer raged uncontrollably—it danced at his feet, a flickering light that illuminated the path ahead.

Finn had passed the trial of fire, proving his ability to harness its power without being consumed by it.

The Trial of Water

The final element awaited Finn in the western section of the clearing. A large, shimmering pool of water lay before him, its surface still and reflective, mirroring the sky above. The air here was cool and calm, a stark contrast to the trials of earth, air, and fire.

Water was the element of life, of healing, but it was also the element of depth, of mystery. It could be calm and gentle, but it could also be fierce and destructive. To pass the trial of water, Finn would need to prove his ability to navigate the unknown, to face the depths of his own emotions and fears.

He approached the edge of the pool, staring into its depths. The water was crystal clear, but as Finn looked closer, he realized that it was much deeper than it appeared. Shadows moved beneath the surface, shifting and swirling like hidden creatures waiting to rise.

The trial of water was a test of introspection, of facing the unknown within oneself. Finn knew that he would have to dive into the pool, to descend into the depths and confront whatever lay beneath.

Taking a deep breath, he stepped into the water. The cool liquid enveloped him, soothing his skin after the heat of the fire. He waded deeper, the water rising to his chest, then his shoulders, until finally, he took one last breath and submerged himself completely.

The world beneath the water was silent, the only sound the steady beat of his heart. The light from the surface grew dimmer as Finn swam deeper, the shadows around him growing darker, more oppressive. He could feel the weight of the water pressing down on him, the cold seeping into his bones.

But Finn did not stop. He swam deeper, his lungs burning for air, his heart pounding in his chest. The water was testing him, pushing him to his limits, forcing him to confront his fears of the unknown, of drowning in the depths of his own mind.

Just when he thought he couldn't go any further, Finn saw a faint light in the distance, glowing softly at the bottom of the pool. He swam toward it, his muscles aching, his lungs screaming for air, but he refused to give up.

Finally, he reached the light, and as he touched it, a wave of warmth washed over him. The water around him grew brighter, and the shadows that had surrounded him faded away. The surface of the pool appeared above him, and with one final effort, Finn swam upward, breaking through the water and gasping for air.

He had passed the trial of water, proving his ability to face the unknown and emerge stronger on the other side.

The Spirits' Favor

As Finn stood at the edge of the clearing, dripping wet but triumphant, the air around him shimmered with a soft, ethereal light. The spirits of the forest had watched his every move, and now, they revealed themselves.

A gentle breeze stirred the leaves, and the ground beneath Finn's feet seemed to hum with life. The flames in the distance flickered softly, and the pool of water glowed with a soft, blue light. The elements had tested him, and he had proven himself worthy.

The spirits spoke to him, their voices like the rustling of leaves, the whisper of wind, the crackle of fire, and the bubbling of water.

"You have passed the Trial of the Elements," they said. "You have proven your understanding of the balance between earth, air, fire, and water. You are worthy of the forest's favor."

Finn bowed his head, his heart filled with gratitude and awe. He had faced the elements, overcome their trials, and earned the favor of the spirits who guarded the Eternal Forest. But more than that, he had gained a deeper understanding of the balance that sustained the world around him.

The trial was over, but Finn knew that his journey was far from complete. There were still more secrets to uncover, more challenges to face. But now, with the favor of the forest's spirits, he felt ready to face whatever lay ahead.

As he left the clearing and stepped back into the forest, Finn carried with him the knowledge that he had been tested by the very forces that shaped the world—and he had emerged stronger than ever before.

Chapter 12: The Gathering of Creatures

Uniting Against a Common Foe

The Eternal Forest had always been a place of harmony, a delicate balance maintained by the ancient magic that coursed through its roots, its trees, and its creatures. The forest was home to many legendary beings—powerful, mystical, and wise—each one contributing to the protection of the forest and ensuring that its secrets remained safeguarded from the outside world. Finn had spent months traversing the forest, gaining the favor of its spirits, and passing the trials that had tested every part of his soul. But now, a dark and imminent threat was brewing, one that could shatter the balance and bring chaos to the entire forest.

The air in the forest had changed, charged with an unsettling tension that rippled through the trees and stirred unease among the creatures. Whispers of the growing danger traveled on the wind, and even the oldest and wisest of the forest dwellers had begun to stir from their hidden sanctuaries. A darkness was spreading, one that threatened to consume the forest in its entirety, and the time had come for the guardians of the Eternal Forest to unite against this common foe.

Finn stood at the edge of the Sacred Grove, the heart of the forest, where the ancient magic was strongest. It was here that the gathering of creatures was to take place—an unprecedented event where the legendary beings of the forest would come together to discuss how best to confront the looming danger. Finn had been tasked with summoning them, with convincing them that only by working together could they stand a chance against what was coming.

He knew it would not be easy. The creatures of the forest were diverse, each with their own interests, their own territories, and their own sense of pride. Some were solitary, preferring the isolation of their hidden realms, while others were more communal, but fiercely protective of their domains. And then there were the more elusive beings, those whose very existence had faded into legend, rarely seen by even the most knowledgeable inhabitants of the forest.

But Finn had no choice. The survival of the forest depended on unity. He had already faced countless challenges in his journey, but this task felt even more daunting than any trial he had endured.

The first of the creatures to arrive was the Phoenix.

Finn felt the air shift before he saw her, the heat radiating from the sky above signaling her approach. He looked up and saw the great bird soaring through the sky, her feathers ablaze with brilliant shades of red, orange, and gold. The Phoenix had become a symbol of renewal, of hope, after Finn had witnessed her rebirth from the ashes. Now, she was flying once more, her wings leaving a trail of shimmering light in her wake.

As she descended gracefully into the Sacred Grove, Finn stepped forward to greet her.

"Thank you for coming," Finn said, bowing his head in respect. "Your presence here means more than you know."

The Phoenix's eyes glowed with an ancient wisdom as she gazed at him. "The forest is in danger," she said, her voice like the crackling of a warm fire. "I could feel it even from the skies. It is time for us to stand together."

Finn nodded, relieved that the Phoenix understood the gravity of the situation. He had always known that the Phoenix would be one of the most important allies in this fight. Her power of rebirth, her ability to rise from the flames of destruction, was a symbol of resilience that the forest desperately needed.

Next to arrive were the Faeries.

Finn sensed their presence before he saw them, a soft fluttering in the air accompanied by the tinkling sound of tiny bells. The Faeries emerged from the trees in a swarm of iridescent wings, their small bodies glowing with an ethereal light. They flitted through the air, giggling and whispering to one another in a language only they understood, their playfulness a stark contrast to the seriousness of the situation.

"Finn!" one of the Faeries cried, flying up to hover in front of his face. She was tiny, no larger than his hand, with delicate wings that shimmered like rainbows in the sunlight. "We heard you were calling a meeting! How exciting! What's the occasion?"

Finn smiled despite the gravity of the moment. The Faeries were mischievous by nature, but they were also deeply connected to the forest, and he knew they would fight fiercely to protect their home. "A darkness is spreading through the forest," he explained. "We need to unite if we're going to stop it."

The Faerie tilted her head, her eyes glowing with curiosity. "Darkness, you say? Well, we don't like the sound of that! We'll help, of course. Anything to keep our forest safe."

With the Faeries' enthusiastic agreement, Finn felt a surge of hope. The Phoenix and the Faeries were powerful allies, but there were still others he needed to convince.

The ground beneath Finn's feet began to tremble slightly, and he knew who was coming next.

The Guardian of the Forest emerged from the shadows of the trees, his massive form towering over the others. He was an ancient being, his body covered in thick bark and moss, his eyes glowing with the light of a thousand years of wisdom. The Guardian had watched over the forest for millennia, maintaining the balance between the creatures and the land. His presence commanded respect, and even the Phoenix and the Faeries grew silent in his presence.

"Guardian," Finn said, bowing deeply. "Thank you for answering the call."

The Guardian's deep voice rumbled through the clearing like the sound of trees creaking in the wind. "The forest is my charge, and I will do whatever is necessary to protect it. This darkness you speak of—it is ancient, older than any of us. It must be stopped."

Finn nodded, his heart heavy with the weight of the Guardian's words. If the Guardian believed the threat was ancient, then it was more dangerous than Finn had realized. He had suspected that the darkness was no ordinary danger, but hearing it from the Guardian himself only confirmed his fears.

As the Guardian took his place in the Sacred Grove, more creatures began to arrive.

The Serpent slithered out from the shadows, its golden eyes gleaming as it coiled its massive body around the base of a tree. Finn had once battled the Serpent, a creature of darkness and cunning, but now they shared a common enemy. The Serpent had agreed to join the fight, not out of loyalty to the forest, but out of a desire to preserve its own power. Despite their uneasy alliance,

Finn knew that the Serpent's knowledge of the forest's dark corners would be invaluable.

From the sky came the Roc, a giant bird of prey whose wings spanned the length of the clearing. The Roc's feathers were a deep midnight blue, and its talons gleamed like polished steel. It landed with a thud, its sharp eyes scanning the gathering below. The Roc was a solitary creature, rarely seen by anyone in the forest, but its strength and speed were unmatched.

Then came the Centaurs, their muscular bodies half-human, half-horse, their bows slung across their backs. The Centaurs were warriors, skilled in both archery and strategy. They were fierce protectors of the forest, and their leader, a tall and stoic Centaur named Theron, approached Finn with a nod of respect.

"We have heard of the darkness," Theron said, his voice deep and steady. "The Centaurs will fight alongside you. The forest has been our home for generations, and we will not let it fall."

Finn bowed his head in gratitude. The Centaurs' prowess in battle would be crucial in the fight to come.

As the creatures gathered, the air in the Sacred Grove buzzed with tension. The Phoenix, the Faeries, the Guardian, the Serpent, the Roc, and the Centaurs—all of them had answered the call. But there were still others Finn hoped would come.

He glanced toward the shadows at the edge of the grove, where the trees seemed to twist and warp in unnatural ways. The Shadows, the elusive beings who lived in the darkest parts of the forest, had not yet arrived. Finn wasn't sure if they would come—they were mysterious, even among the creatures of the forest, and their motives were often unclear. But if they could be convinced to join the fight, their ability to move unseen through the darkness would be invaluable.

As if in response to his thoughts, a figure stepped out of the shadows.

She was tall and graceful, her skin the color of the night sky, her eyes glowing like stars. She moved with an ethereal grace, her form shifting and shimmering as if she were made of the very shadows that surrounded her. She was one of the Shadowkin, the ancient beings who had lived in the deepest parts of the forest for as long as anyone could remember.

"You seek our aid," she said, her voice soft and melodic, yet filled with power. "The darkness that threatens the forest is not unfamiliar to us. We have seen it before, long ago."

Finn stepped forward, his heart pounding. "Will you help us?"

The Shadowkin woman studied him for a long moment, her glowing eyes piercing through him. Finally, she nodded. "We will fight. The forest is our home, and we will not let it be consumed by the darkness."

With the Shadowkin's agreement, the gathering was complete. The legendary creatures of the forest—the Phoenix, the Faeries, the Guardian, the Serpent, the Roc, the Centaurs, and the Shadowkin—had all come together, united by the common goal of protecting the forest from the growing threat.

Finn stood at the center of the Sacred Grove, surrounded by the most powerful beings in the forest, and yet he felt the weight of the task ahead pressing down on him. They had gathered, but now they had to decide how to fight.

The darkness was spreading, and time was running out.

The Council of War

As the creatures took their places in the grove, Finn realized that the next challenge would be forging a plan that could bring all these diverse beings together. The forest was vast, and the threat was elusive. It was not a single enemy that they could fight face-to-face, but a creeping force that threatened the balance of the entire ecosystem.

"We need to understand what this darkness is," Finn began, addressing the gathering. "The Guardian has said that it's ancient, older than any of us. What exactly are we dealing with?"

The Guardian of the Forest stepped forward, his massive form casting a long shadow over the group. "The darkness is not a creature or an enemy in the traditional sense. It is a force, a corruption of the natural order. Long ago, before even I came to this forest, there were those who sought to harness the magic of the land for their own purposes. They delved too deep, sought too much power, and in doing so, they unleashed something terrible."

The Phoenix's wings flared as she spoke. "The Eternal Flame has felt the shift in the balance. The darkness is growing stronger, feeding off the very magic that sustains the forest. If we do not act soon, it will consume everything."

The Faeries, who had been darting about playfully just moments before, grew still, their expressions serious. "We've seen the shadows creeping closer," one of them said. "The trees are whispering of strange happenings—flowers wilting, streams drying up. The forest is sick."

Finn nodded, his mind racing. The darkness wasn't just an external threat—it was corrupting the very magic of the forest itself. If they didn't stop it, it would destroy the forest from the inside out.

"But how do we fight something like that?" Theron, the leader of the Centaurs, asked. "We cannot shoot arrows at a force of nature."

Finn turned to the Serpent, whose golden eyes gleamed with cunning. "You know the darker parts of the forest better than anyone. What have you seen?"

The Serpent's tongue flicked out as he considered his words. "The darkness is drawn to places of power. The ancient ley lines that run through the forest are its target. It seeks to corrupt them, to break the balance and unleash chaos."

Finn's mind raced. The ley lines—the magical veins that ran beneath the forest, connecting its sacred places—were the source of the forest's strength. If the darkness was targeting them, then they needed to protect those places at all costs.

"The ley lines," Finn said, his voice urgent. "We need to protect the ley lines. If the darkness corrupts them, the forest will fall."

The Guardian nodded. "You are right. The ley lines must be defended, but we cannot be everywhere at once. We will need to split our forces, to guard each of the sacred places where the ley lines converge."

Finn looked around the gathering. The Phoenix, the Faeries, the Centaurs, the Serpent, the Roc, the Shadowkin—they were powerful, but they were few. They would need to divide their strength if they were going to protect the forest's sacred places.

"We'll need to work together," Finn said. "Each of you has unique strengths—use them. The Phoenix, you and the Roc can take to the skies, watching for any signs of the darkness spreading. The Faeries can travel quickly through the trees, warning us of any disturbances. The Centaurs are skilled warriors—they can defend the sacred groves on the ground. The Serpent knows the hidden places of the forest better than anyone—you can track the darkness to its source. And the Shadowkin..." Finn paused, turning to the shadowy figure who stood at the edge of the group. "You move unseen through the darkest parts of the forest. You'll be our eyes where the darkness is strongest."

The Shadowkin woman nodded, her glowing eyes unreadable. "We will watch from the shadows. But be warned—the darkness is clever. It will try to deceive us, to turn us against each other."

Finn clenched his fists, his mind already racing with strategies. "Then we must stay united. The darkness thrives on division, on chaos. If we stand together, we can defeat it."

There was a moment of silence as the creatures considered Finn's words. The forest's greatest defenders had gathered, but they were all aware of the gravity of the situation. This was no ordinary battle—it was a fight for the very soul of the Eternal Forest.

Finally, the Guardian spoke. "We will defend the forest," he rumbled. "We will protect the ley lines, and we will drive the darkness back."

The Phoenix flared her wings, the flames glowing brightly in the gathering dusk. "The forest will not fall," she declared. "We will rise from the ashes if need be."

Theron, the leader of the Centaurs, drew his bow, his expression fierce. "We will stand together. For the forest."

The Faeries, usually so lighthearted, hovered in the air, their faces set with determination. "The forest is our home. We'll fight to protect it."

The Serpent coiled around the base of the tree, his golden eyes gleaming with anticipation. "The darkness will regret ever setting foot in this forest."

The Shadowkin woman melted back into the shadows, her voice a whisper on the wind. "We are with you."

Finn took a deep breath, his heart pounding in his chest. The gathering had come together, and now, they were ready to face the darkness.

The fight for the Eternal Forest had begun.

Chapter 13: The Battle for the Eternal Forest

The Final Confrontation

The Eternal Forest, once serene and balanced, now thrummed with an ominous energy. Every leaf, every tree, every creature seemed to sense the impending storm of conflict that would determine the fate of their world. The ley lines, the very veins of magic that coursed beneath the forest's surface, pulsed with a dim, erratic light, as if struggling against the encroaching darkness. This was the moment the forest had dreaded for centuries—the final confrontation between light and shadow, between the defenders of the forest and the dark forces led by the Serpent.

Finn stood at the edge of the Sacred Grove, his heart pounding as he surveyed the assembled forces. The creatures he had gathered—the Phoenix, the Faeries, the Centaurs, the Roc, the Guardian of the Forest, the Shadowkin, and the Serpent—were all prepared to face the oncoming threat. But even as they stood united, Finn could feel the weight of uncertainty hanging over them.

The Serpent, once an uneasy ally, had turned on them. The ancient creature had always been driven by ambition and cunning, and now it sought to claim the power of the Eternal Forest for itself. It had allied with the forces of darkness, unleashing a horde of shadowy creatures that had begun to corrupt the forest's magic, slowly unraveling the delicate balance that had sustained the land for millennia.

The battle for the Eternal Forest was about to begin, and Finn knew that the stakes couldn't be higher. If they failed, the forest would fall into darkness, its magic twisted and consumed by the Serpent's ambition. But if they succeeded, they would restore the balance and protect the forest for generations to come.

He turned to the Phoenix, who stood beside him, her wings glowing with the radiant light of the Eternal Flame. Her fiery presence filled the air with warmth and hope, but there was also a sense of grim determination in her eyes. The Faeries flitted nervously above, their tiny bodies glowing with an iridescent light, while the Guardian loomed silently in the background, his massive form a testament to the forest's strength and resilience.

"We're ready," Finn said, his voice steady despite the fear gnawing at him.

The Phoenix nodded, her eyes glowing with intensity. "We must act swiftly. The darkness is already spreading—if we don't stop it soon, the ley lines will be completely corrupted."

Finn glanced at the others. The Centaurs stood in a tight formation, their bows at the ready, while the Shadowkin moved silently through the shadows, their forms shifting and blending with the darkened forest. The Roc circled above, its sharp eyes scanning the horizon for any sign of the approaching enemy.

"The Serpent will strike soon," Finn said, his gaze sweeping across the clearing. "We need to divide our forces to protect the ley lines. The Phoenix and the Roc will guard the skies. The Centaurs and I will defend the ley lines on the ground. The Faeries and the Shadowkin can move quickly through the forest—use that to your advantage to scout and relay information."

The Guardian rumbled in agreement, his voice like the deep creaking of ancient trees. "I will guard the Sacred Grove. This place must not fall."

As they finalized their strategy, a low hiss echoed through the forest, sending a shiver down Finn's spine. It was a sound he recognized all too well—the voice of the Serpent. The ground trembled beneath his feet, and the trees seemed to sway as if recoiling from the darkness that was drawing near.

"They're coming," the Faerie leader whispered, her wings fluttering anxiously.

Finn tightened his grip on his sword, his eyes narrowing as he looked toward the horizon. Dark figures were moving through the trees, their shapes indistinct but filled with malice. The creatures of shadow had arrived, and they were not alone. Twisted and deformed, the creatures resembled monstrous versions of the forest's own inhabitants—wolves with glowing red eyes, serpents made of black mist, and hulking beasts whose forms shifted and flickered as if they were made of living shadows.

At the center of the approaching horde was the Serpent.

Its massive body slithered through the trees, its scales gleaming with an unnatural light. Its golden eyes, once cunning and calculating, were now filled with a hunger for power that chilled Finn to the core. The Serpent had grown larger since Finn had last seen it, its body coiled with dark magic, and it moved with a terrible grace as it led the army of darkness toward the Sacred Grove.

The battle had begun.

The Skirmish at the Sacred Grove

The air crackled with tension as the defenders of the Eternal Forest braced themselves for the onslaught. The Serpent's army surged forward, their shadowy forms spreading like a plague through the trees. The first wave of creatures crashed into the forest's defenders, and chaos erupted.

Finn was at the front, his sword flashing in the dim light as he met the charge head-on. The creatures of shadow snarled and snapped at him, their teeth gleaming like jagged shards of darkness. He slashed at them, his blade cutting through their insubstantial forms, but for every creature he felled, two more seemed to take its place.

To his right, the Centaurs fought with the precision of seasoned warriors. Their arrows flew through the air in a deadly rain, each shot finding its mark in the heart of the advancing horde. Theron, the leader of the Centaurs, stood tall in the midst of the battle, his bow drawn and ready as he commanded his warriors with calm authority.

The Faeries darted through the trees, their tiny forms nearly invisible as they zipped between the branches. They unleashed bursts of magic that crackled like lightning, stunning the shadow creatures and leaving them vulnerable to the Centaurs' arrows. Their laughter, once playful and light, was now filled with a fierce determination.

Above, the Phoenix and the Roc engaged the Serpent's forces in the sky. The Phoenix's wings blazed with fire as she dove into the midst of the shadow creatures, her flames burning away the darkness with every strike. The Roc, its talons sharp as steel, tore through the air with lethal precision, its massive wings beating back the creatures that dared to challenge it.

But even as the defenders held their ground, the Serpent's forces continued to press forward, relentless and unyielding. The darkness was spreading, and

Finn could feel the corruption seeping into the forest, its tendrils reaching for the ley lines that lay beneath the ground.

"We're being overrun!" one of the Centaurs shouted, his voice barely audible over the din of battle.

Finn gritted his teeth, slashing through another shadow creature as he glanced around the battlefield. They couldn't hold the line forever—there were simply too many enemies. And the Serpent, the true source of the darkness, had yet to make its move.

"We need to get to the ley lines!" Finn shouted. "We can't let them reach the sacred places!"

Theron nodded, his eyes fierce as he pulled another arrow from his quiver. "We'll hold them off as long as we can."

Finn turned to the Faeries, who were flitting about in the trees, their magic illuminating the darkness. "Go! Find the ley lines and protect them!"

The Faeries nodded and scattered, their wings glowing as they sped through the forest, racing to defend the ley lines from the encroaching darkness. Finn could only hope that they would be fast enough.

The Serpent Strikes

As the battle raged on, the ground beneath Finn's feet began to tremble. A low, rumbling hiss filled the air, and Finn's heart skipped a beat as he realized what was happening.

The Serpent was moving.

Its massive form slithered through the trees, crushing everything in its path as it made its way toward the Sacred Grove. Its eyes gleamed with malice, and the dark magic that radiated from its body seemed to warp the very air around it.

"We have to stop it!" Finn shouted, turning to the Phoenix. "If the Serpent reaches the ley lines, the forest is finished!"

The Phoenix's eyes blazed with determination as she spread her wings. "I will hold the Serpent back. But you must find a way to sever its connection to the darkness."

Finn nodded, his mind racing. The Serpent was the source of the corruption, the anchor that was allowing the darkness to spread. If they could sever its connection to the dark magic, they might be able to weaken it enough to defeat it.

But how?

The Serpent's power had grown since Finn's last encounter with it. It was no longer just a cunning creature of the forest—it had become a vessel for the darkness, a living embodiment of the corruption that threatened to consume everything.

As Finn considered his options, the Serpent struck.

With terrifying speed, it lashed out with its massive tail, sending several Centaurs flying through the air. It reared back, its jaws opening wide as it let out a deafening roar that shook the very trees. The air around it darkened, and Finn could feel the oppressive weight of the dark magic pressing down on him.

The Phoenix dove toward the Serpent, her wings blazing with fire as she unleashed a torrent of flames. The fire engulfed the Serpent, but instead of recoiling, the creature seemed to absorb the flames, its scales glowing with an eerie light as the fire was drawn into its body.

"The Serpent is feeding off the magic!" Finn realized with a start. "It's using the power of the forest against us!"

The Serpent's eyes gleamed with triumph as it lashed out again, its body coiling and uncoiling with terrifying grace. The Phoenix barely dodged the attack, her wings singed by the dark energy that radiated from the Serpent's scales.

"We need to sever its connection to the ley lines!" Finn shouted, his mind racing as he searched for a solution.

The ley lines—the magical veins that ran beneath the forest—were the key. The Serpent was drawing its power from them, using the ancient magic to fuel its dark transformation. If they could disrupt that connection, they might be able to weaken the Serpent enough to defeat it.

But how could they sever a force as ancient and powerful as the ley lines themselves?

A Desperate Plan

As Finn struggled to think of a solution, a voice echoed in his mind—the voice of the Guardian of the Forest.

"The ley lines are ancient, but they can be redirected. The magic that flows through them is not fixed—it is a living force, and it responds to the will of the forest."

Finn's eyes widened as he realized what the Guardian was suggesting. If they could redirect the flow of magic through the ley lines, they could cut off the Serpent's access to the power it was feeding on. But doing so would require immense focus and control—more than Finn had ever attempted before.

"I'll need your help," Finn said, turning to the Guardian. "We need to redirect the ley lines, but I can't do it alone."

The Guardian nodded, his massive form looming over the battlefield as he extended his hand toward the ground. "I will lend you my strength. But be warned—this will not be easy. The ley lines are deeply entrenched in the forest's magic. It will take everything we have to shift them."

Finn swallowed hard, feeling the weight of the task ahead. But there was no other choice. If they didn't stop the Serpent now, the forest would be lost.

With a deep breath, Finn knelt down and placed his hands on the ground, focusing on the energy that flowed beneath the surface. He could feel the pulse of the ley lines, the ancient magic coursing through the earth like a river of light. It was strong, powerful, but it was also chaotic—shifting and flowing in unpredictable ways.

The Guardian knelt beside him, his hands glowing with a soft, green light as he reached out to the ley lines. Together, they began to focus their energy, trying to guide the flow of magic away from the Serpent.

At first, it was like trying to move a mountain. The ley lines resisted their efforts, the magic pushing back with a force that nearly knocked Finn off balance. But he gritted his teeth and pressed on, his mind locked on the task at hand.

Slowly, painfully, they began to shift the flow of magic. The ley lines trembled, their light flickering as the energy began to redirect itself. Finn could feel the strain on his body, the immense pressure of the magic pressing down on him, but he refused to give up.

"Almost there..." the Guardian rumbled, his voice strained with effort.

The Serpent let out a roar of rage as it felt the ley lines shifting beneath it. Its body convulsed, the dark magic flickering and sputtering as its connection to the ley lines was disrupted.

"We're doing it!" Finn shouted, his voice filled with hope.

But just as they were about to sever the Serpent's connection completely, the ground beneath them erupted in a wave of dark energy. The Serpent, sensing its defeat, unleashed a final, desperate attack, its body coiling and writhing as it released the full force of its dark power.

Finn was thrown back, the force of the blast sending him crashing into the ground. His vision blurred, and for a moment, he thought he had failed.

But then, as the dust began to settle, he saw the Serpent.

Its body was convulsing, its scales flickering with dark energy as it writhed in pain. The ley lines, now fully severed, no longer fed it the magic it had been consuming. The darkness that had once fueled it was now turning against it, consuming it from within.

The Serpent let out one final, anguished roar before its massive body collapsed, its form dissolving into a cloud of black mist that quickly dissipated into the air.

The battle was over.

The Aftermath

The forest was silent.

The shadow creatures, once so fierce and relentless, had vanished along with the Serpent. The darkness that had spread through the trees was slowly receding, and the ley lines, though weakened, were beginning to heal.

Finn lay on the ground, his body aching and his mind exhausted, but he felt a deep sense of relief. They had won. The Serpent was defeated, and the forest was safe.

The Phoenix landed beside him, her wings glowing softly in the fading light. "You did it," she said, her voice filled with warmth and pride. "The forest is saved."

Finn smiled weakly, his chest heaving as he struggled to catch his breath. "We did it," he corrected, glancing around at the other creatures who had fought alongside him. The Centaurs, the Faeries, the Roc, the Shadowkin, the Guardian—they had all played a part in the battle, and without their help, they never would have succeeded.

As the creatures gathered around him, Finn felt a deep sense of gratitude. The forest had tested him, pushed him to his limits, but it had also given him the strength to face the darkness and emerge victorious.

The Eternal Forest, once again, stood tall.

And though the scars of the battle would take time to heal, Finn knew that the forest would endure, just as it always had. It was a place of balance, of light and shadow, and that balance had been restored.

For now.

Chapter 14: The Dawn of a New Era
Restoring Balance

The Eternal Forest had always been a place of mystery and wonder, a realm where ancient magic wove its way through the trees, and the creatures that called it home lived in a delicate balance of light and shadow. But now, in the aftermath of the battle against the Serpent and the dark forces that had threatened to consume the forest, the air felt different. It was lighter, calmer, as if the very essence of the forest had breathed a collective sigh of relief.

The sky was still dark, the remnants of the night clinging to the horizon, but a soft glow of dawn began to rise, casting the first rays of light over the canopy of trees. It was the dawn of a new era, one born from struggle and sacrifice. The forest was safe, for now, and the creatures that had defended it were scattered throughout the Sacred Grove, tending to their wounds, reflecting on the battle, and preparing for what came next.

Finn stood alone at the edge of the Sacred Grove, his gaze fixed on the horizon as the first light of day crept into the sky. His body was weary, his muscles sore from the battle, but his heart was filled with a deep sense of peace. The Serpent, the ancient creature of darkness that had sought to claim the power of the Eternal Forest, was gone. Its army of shadowy creatures had been defeated, and the darkness that had threatened to corrupt the forest's magic had receded.

But the victory had not come without a cost. The forest had suffered, its magic strained and its creatures tested beyond their limits. The ley lines, the magical veins that ran beneath the forest and connected its sacred places, had been disrupted during the battle, and though they were beginning to heal, the process would take time. The balance that had sustained the forest for millennia was fragile, and it would require careful tending to ensure that it was fully restored.

As Finn stood there, lost in thought, he felt a presence beside him. He turned to see the Phoenix, her fiery wings glowing softly in the dawn light. She had been a beacon of hope during the battle, her power of rebirth symbolizing the resilience of the forest and its ability to rise from the ashes of destruction.

"You did well," the Phoenix said, her voice warm and gentle. "The forest owes you a great debt."

Finn shook his head, a humble smile on his lips. "I didn't do it alone. We all played our part. The forest would not have survived without everyone coming together."

The Phoenix's eyes glowed with approval. "True. But you were the one who united us, the one who believed that we could overcome the darkness by standing together. That takes more than strength—it takes wisdom and heart."

Finn looked out at the forest, his thoughts drifting back to the journey that had brought him here. When he had first entered the Eternal Forest, he had been a simple traveler, curious about the mysteries of the land and eager to uncover its secrets. He had never imagined that he would one day stand here, a hero who had helped to save the forest from annihilation. The trials he had faced, the creatures he had met, the battles he had fought—they had all shaped him, tested him, and made him stronger.

But more than that, they had taught him the importance of balance. The forest was not just a place of beauty and magic—it was a living entity, a delicate ecosystem where every creature, every tree, every breath of wind played a role in maintaining harmony. The battle against the Serpent had been a stark reminder of what happened when that balance was threatened, and now, as the forest began to heal, Finn knew that it was his duty to help protect that balance.

The Phoenix extended one of her wings, brushing it lightly against Finn's shoulder. "You've come a long way," she said, her voice soft. "But your journey is not over. The forest is healing, but it will need your guidance in the days to come. There are still many challenges ahead."

Finn nodded, his heart filled with a sense of purpose. "I'll be here," he said, his voice steady. "I won't let the forest fall into darkness again."

As the Phoenix spread her wings and soared into the sky, her fiery form glowing against the pale light of dawn, Finn turned back toward the Sacred Grove. The creatures of the forest had gathered there, their faces a mixture of relief and exhaustion. The Centaurs, led by Theron, were tending to their wounded, their stoic expressions softened by the knowledge that the battle had been won. The Faeries flitted through the trees, their laughter once again light and playful as they darted between the branches. The Roc circled high above, its keen eyes scanning the horizon for any remaining threats.

The Guardian of the Forest stood at the center of the grove, his massive form a symbol of the forest's strength and endurance. His bark-covered body was scarred from the battle, but his eyes glowed with a deep, unshakable resolve. He had watched over the forest for millennia, and now, with the Serpent defeated, he would continue to protect it for generations to come.

As Finn approached, the Guardian turned to him, his deep voice rumbling like the creaking of ancient trees. "The forest is safe, thanks to you," he said, his words filled with reverence. "But there is much work to be done. The ley lines are weakened, and the magic of the forest is still fragile. It will take time to restore the balance."

Finn nodded, his mind already racing with thoughts of how to help the forest heal. "What can I do?" he asked, his voice filled with determination.

The Guardian placed a hand on Finn's shoulder, his touch surprisingly gentle for such a massive being. "You have already done much," he said. "But there is more to be done. The ley lines must be nurtured, their magic restored. The creatures of the forest must be protected, and the balance between light and shadow must be maintained. It will not be easy, but I believe you are up to the task."

Finn took a deep breath, feeling the weight of responsibility settle on his shoulders. He had fought for the forest, but now he would have to learn how to care for it in a different way. The battle had been won, but the true work of restoring balance was only just beginning.

The Healing of the Ley Lines

The ley lines were the lifeblood of the Eternal Forest, invisible rivers of magic that connected the sacred places and sustained the forest's power. During the battle, the Serpent had drawn its strength from these ley lines, corrupting their magic and disrupting the balance that had kept the forest in harmony for so long. Now, with the darkness vanquished, it was time to repair the damage and restore the ley lines to their full strength.

Finn stood at one of the ley line convergences, a place where the magic was strongest. The ground beneath his feet hummed with energy, but it was a faint, flickering pulse, like the heartbeat of someone who had been gravely wounded. The trees around him were still, their leaves drooping as if they, too, were feeling the effects of the weakened magic.

The Guardian stood beside him, his ancient wisdom guiding the process. "The ley lines are delicate," he said, his voice low and calm. "They are not like rivers that can be dammed or diverted with force. They respond to the will of the forest, to the natural order. We must be gentle, patient."

Finn knelt down, placing his hands on the ground. He closed his eyes and focused on the energy beneath the surface, feeling the faint pulse of the ley lines as they struggled to regain their strength. He could sense the damage that had been done—the magic was fractured, disjointed, as if pieces of it had been torn away during the battle.

But he could also feel the potential for healing. The ley lines were not broken beyond repair—they were simply in need of guidance, of nurturing. It was like tending to a wounded animal, coaxing it back to health with care and patience.

As Finn focused his energy on the ley lines, he felt the Guardian's presence beside him, a steady, grounding force that helped to anchor the magic. Together, they began to channel their energy into the ley lines, not forcing them to heal, but encouraging them, gently guiding the magic back into its proper flow.

It was a slow process, and at times, it felt as though they were making no progress at all. But Finn remained patient, his hands steady as he continued to focus on the task at hand. Slowly, the pulse of the ley lines began to grow stronger, the magic flowing more smoothly beneath the surface.

The trees around them began to stir, their leaves lifting as if they were waking from a long slumber. The air grew warmer, the scent of fresh earth and blooming flowers filling the air. The forest was healing.

After what felt like hours, Finn opened his eyes and looked at the Guardian. The ancient being's face was serene, his eyes glowing with approval.

"The ley lines are healing," the Guardian said softly. "The balance is being restored."

Finn nodded, his heart swelling with a sense of accomplishment. He could feel the difference in the air, in the very fabric of the forest. The magic was returning, slowly but surely, and with it, the forest was beginning to come back to life.

A New Beginning

As the days passed, the forest continued to heal. The creatures that had fought in the battle returned to their homes, their spirits lifted by the knowledge that they had saved the forest from destruction. The Centaurs patrolled the edges of the forest, keeping watch for any signs of lingering darkness, while the Faeries flitted through the trees, spreading

joy and laughter wherever they went.

The Phoenix, true to her nature, had risen from the ashes of the battle stronger than ever. Her flames burned brighter, her wings spreading warmth and light throughout the forest. She had become a symbol of hope for the creatures of the forest, a reminder that no matter how dark the times may seem, there is always the possibility of renewal.

The Roc, though more solitary by nature, had also taken on a new role in the aftermath of the battle. It soared high above the forest, its sharp eyes watching for any signs of danger. Its presence was a reassuring one, a reminder that the forest was protected from threats both seen and unseen.

The Shadowkin, elusive as ever, had retreated back into the darkest corners of the forest, their role in the battle complete. But Finn knew that they were always watching, always ready to step forward if the balance of the forest was threatened once again.

As for Finn, he had found a new sense of purpose. He was no longer just a traveler, wandering through the forest in search of adventure. He had become a protector, a guardian of the balance that sustained the Eternal Forest. The trials he had faced, the battles he had fought, had shaped him into someone who understood the importance of harmony, of working with the natural world rather than against it.

He spent his days walking through the forest, tending to the ley lines, helping the creatures rebuild their homes, and ensuring that the balance between light and shadow remained intact. It was hard work, but it was also fulfilling, and Finn knew that he had found his place in the world.

One morning, as the sun rose over the forest, casting its golden light over the trees, Finn stood at the edge of the Sacred Grove and reflected on his journey. The forest, once threatened by darkness, was now thriving once again. The ley lines were strong, the creatures were at peace, and the magic of the forest flowed freely through the land.

But more than that, Finn had come to understand the true nature of the Eternal Forest. It was not just a place of magic and beauty—it was a living entity, one that required care and attention to maintain its delicate balance. The creatures that called it home were not just inhabitants—they were part of the forest's ecosystem, each one playing a role in its survival.

The dawn of a new era had arrived, and with it, the promise of a brighter future for the Eternal Forest. But Finn knew that the work of maintaining balance was never truly finished. There would always be challenges, always be threats to the forest's harmony. But now, with the lessons he had learned and the strength of the creatures beside him, Finn felt ready to face whatever the future held.

The Eternal Forest, once again, stood strong.

And so did Finn.

The Legacy of the Eternal Forest

The story of the battle for the Eternal Forest would be passed down through the generations, told by the Faeries in their songs and whispered by the trees as the wind rustled through their leaves. The Phoenix's flames would continue to burn bright, a symbol of hope and renewal for all who lived within the forest's bounds. The ley lines, now healed and strong, would once again serve as the lifeblood of the forest, connecting the sacred places and ensuring that the magic flowed freely through the land.

And Finn, the traveler who had become a hero, would always be remembered as the one who had united the creatures of the forest in their darkest hour, who had fought to protect the balance and restore the magic that sustained the Eternal Forest.

But more than that, Finn's legacy would live on in the hearts of the creatures who had fought beside him, in the trees that swayed gently in the wind, and in the very magic that flowed through the ley lines. He had become a part of the forest, just as the forest had become a part of him.

As the first light of dawn bathed the forest in its golden glow, Finn smiled, his heart filled with peace.

The battle had been won, the balance restored.

And the Eternal Forest, in all its beauty and magic, would endure.

Chapter 15: The Legacy of the Eternal Forest

Passing Down the Legend

The Eternal Forest had become more than just a destination for Finn—it had transformed into a place of deep understanding, a living entity that had shaped him into someone entirely different from the young traveler who had first ventured into its depths. He had entered the forest seeking adventure, curious about the legends and mysteries that swirled around it, but now, standing at the forest's edge, ready to leave, he carried with him something far greater. He was leaving not just with tales of magic and wonder, but with profound lessons about balance, unity, and the responsibility to preserve the natural world.

The sky was clear, the golden light of the setting sun casting a soft glow over the treetops. The air felt warm, filled with the earthy scent of pine and moss. The Eternal Forest was once again at peace, its creatures resuming their lives in harmony, its magic restored and flowing freely through the ley lines that ran beneath the earth. But as the tranquility of the forest wrapped around him, Finn felt a bittersweet pang in his heart. It was time to return to the outside world.

The journey had been long and perilous, but it had also been transformative. Finn had faced trials that tested every part of his being—his strength, his courage, his wisdom—and now, on the cusp of leaving, he realized that the true gift the forest had given him was the knowledge of how to live in harmony with the world. The legends and creatures of the forest were not just stories to be told—they were symbols of the delicate balance that governed all of life, a balance that, if disrupted, could lead to chaos and destruction. It was a lesson that needed to be carried forward, a message that needed to be passed down so that future generations would understand the importance of preserving not just the forest, but the world as a whole.

As Finn prepared to take his first steps away from the Sacred Grove, the Phoenix appeared beside him, her wings glowing softly in the fading light. She had been a constant companion during the journey, a symbol of hope and renewal, and now, she stood with him at the threshold of his departure.

"You're leaving," she said, her voice gentle and filled with understanding. It was not a question, but a simple statement of fact.

Finn nodded, his gaze lingering on the trees that stretched out before him. "It's time," he said quietly. "The forest is safe now. The balance has been restored. But there are others who need to hear this story, who need to understand what the forest stands for."

The Phoenix's eyes glowed with approval. "The story of the Eternal Forest is an ancient one, and it has been passed down through many generations. But each time it is told, it takes on new meaning, new significance. You are part of that legacy now, Finn. You carry the wisdom of the forest with you, and it is your duty to ensure that its message is preserved."

Finn felt the weight of her words settle on him, not as a burden, but as a calling. He had been chosen by the forest, not just to protect it in its time of need, but to carry its story to the world beyond. The creatures of the forest, the battles they had fought, the lessons he had learned—all of it would be lost if it was not shared, if the legend of the Eternal Forest faded into obscurity.

"I won't forget," Finn said, his voice filled with quiet resolve. "I'll make sure the story is told. The forest will not be forgotten."

The Phoenix nodded, her fiery feathers glowing more brightly for a moment before she spread her wings and took flight, her form disappearing into the sky. Finn watched her go, his heart filled with gratitude for the journey they had shared. The Phoenix was a symbol of rebirth, of rising from the ashes, and in many ways, Finn felt that he, too, had been reborn through his time in the forest.

Leaving the Forest Behind

The path back to the outside world was not as daunting as Finn had expected it to be. As he walked, the trees parted before him, their branches swaying gently in the breeze as if bidding him farewell. The creatures of the forest, too, seemed to acknowledge his departure. A group of Faeries flitted by, their laughter light and musical, while a majestic stag stood at a distance, watching him with calm, wise eyes. Even the wind seemed to carry with it the whispers of the forest, a soft reminder that although he was leaving, the forest would always be with him.

Finn's heart ached at the thought of leaving behind the creatures and the world that had become so familiar to him. He had fought alongside them, learned from them, and grown in ways he had never imagined. But he knew that his journey was not truly ending—it was simply taking a new direction. The outside world was in need of the lessons the Eternal Forest had to offer, and Finn was determined to be the one to carry that message forward.

As he approached the forest's edge, the landscape began to shift. The dense canopy of trees gave way to rolling hills, the shadows of the forest receding as the open sky stretched out before him. Finn paused for a moment, looking back at the forest one last time. The sight of it, bathed in the golden light of the setting sun, filled him with a deep sense of peace. The forest, with all its magic and mystery, would endure.

But as he turned to leave, he knew that the true test of the forest's legacy would not be in the battles that had been fought, but in the stories that were told. The legends of the Eternal Forest had to be passed down, shared with those who would come after, so that the wisdom of the forest could continue to guide and inspire future generations.

Sharing the Legend

The journey back to civilization was a quiet one. Finn's thoughts were consumed with memories of the forest—the creatures he had met, the battles he had fought, the lessons he had learned. But even as he reflected on his journey, he knew that the real challenge lay ahead. How could he convey the depth of what he had experienced? How could he capture the magic and mystery of the forest in words that others would understand?

The outside world, with its bustling towns and noisy cities, seemed so far removed from the quiet wisdom of the forest. People hurried about their lives, consumed with their own concerns, unaware of the ancient magic that still pulsed beneath the surface of the earth. Finn had once been like them—curious about the world but unaware of the deeper forces that shaped it. Now, he carried the weight of that knowledge with him, and it was up to him to share it.

His first stop was a small village on the outskirts of the forest. The people there had always been wary of the Eternal Forest, viewing it as a place of danger and mystery, a place where only the bravest or most foolish ventured. Finn knew that if he was going to pass down the legend of the forest, he would have to start by dispelling those fears.

He found a small tavern in the village, its walls lined with worn wooden tables and the scent of ale heavy in the air. The villagers gathered there in the evenings, sharing stories and laughter, and it was the perfect place for Finn to begin his tale.

As he sat down at a table near the hearth, he drew the attention of a few curious onlookers. They recognized him as a traveler, someone who had ventured into the forest and returned—a rare feat in itself.

One of the villagers, a grizzled man with a weathered face, approached him. "You've been to the forest, haven't you?" the man asked, his voice rough but curious. "What did you see?"

Finn smiled, gesturing for the man to sit. "I've seen things you wouldn't believe," he said, his voice calm but filled with a quiet intensity. "The Eternal Forest is not what you think it is. It's not a place of danger—it's a place of balance, of magic. And it holds lessons that the world needs to hear."

The man's eyes widened in surprise, and soon, others began to gather around the table, eager to hear more. Finn could see the skepticism in their faces, the disbelief that such a place could exist, but he also saw a flicker of curiosity. These were people who had lived near the forest their entire lives, but they had never truly understood it. They had heard the legends, but they had never seen the truth behind them.

And so, Finn began to tell the story of the Eternal Forest.

He spoke of the creatures that called it home—the majestic Phoenix, the cunning Serpent, the wise Guardian of the Forest. He described the trials he had faced, the battles he had fought, and the lessons he had learned about the importance of balance and unity. He told them of the ley lines, the invisible veins of magic that ran beneath the forest, connecting its sacred places and ensuring that the magic flowed freely through the land.

As he spoke, the villagers listened in rapt silence, their skepticism slowly giving way to awe. They had heard stories of the Eternal Forest before, but never like this. Finn's words painted a picture of a world that was both magical and real, a place that was not just the stuff of legend, but a living, breathing entity that required care and respect.

"The forest isn't just a place," Finn said, his voice growing softer as he neared the end of his tale. "It's a living thing. It has its own magic, its own balance. And if we don't respect that balance, if we don't protect it, the forest will wither. But if we care for it, if we learn from it, it will thrive. And so will we."

The villagers sat in stunned silence for a moment, processing what they had just heard. Finally, the grizzled man who had first approached Finn spoke.

"I've lived near the forest my whole life," he said, his voice thick with emotion. "But I've never really understood it. Not like that."

Finn smiled, feeling a sense of satisfaction settle over him. The story of the Eternal Forest had begun to take root, and he knew that it would continue to grow, spreading from village to village, from person to person.

The Power of Story

Over the next few weeks, Finn traveled from village to village, town to town, sharing the story of the Eternal Forest with anyone who would listen. In taverns, in marketplaces, by the firesides of strangers' homes, he told the tale of the forest's magic, of the battle to protect it, and of the lessons it had taught him.

At first, there were always skeptics—people who believed the forest was nothing more than a dangerous, wild place, filled with creatures that would do them harm. But as Finn spoke, as he shared the depth of his experiences, something began to change. People started to listen, not just with their ears, but with their hearts. They began to see the forest not as a place to fear, but as a place of wonder, a place that held wisdom and beauty beyond their understanding.

In each village he visited, Finn saw the impact of his story. People began to speak of the forest with reverence, with curiosity, and with a newfound respect for the natural world. Children gathered around him, their eyes wide with wonder as they imagined the creatures of the forest—the Phoenix rising from the ashes, the Faeries darting through the trees, the Guardian standing watch over the Sacred Grove.

And with each telling of the story, Finn felt the weight of the legacy he was carrying. The Eternal Forest had given him its wisdom, its magic, and now it was his responsibility to ensure that the legend was preserved.

But it wasn't just the words of the story that mattered—it was the lessons behind them. The importance of balance, of unity, of caring for the natural world. These were lessons that the world needed to hear, now more than ever.

A New Generation of Protectors

As Finn continued to share the story of the Eternal Forest, something unexpected began to happen. People started to seek him out—not just to hear the story, but to learn from him. They wanted to know how they could help protect the forest, how they could carry forward the lessons he had learned.

Farmers asked him how to work with the land in harmony, rather than trying to bend it to their will. Healers wanted to understand the magic of the forest's plants and herbs, to use them for the benefit of their communities. And young travelers, inspired by Finn's tale, set out on their own journeys to discover the magic of the natural world.

Finn realized that the legacy of the Eternal Forest wasn't just about preserving the story—it was about inspiring others to take up the mantle of protector. The forest had given him its wisdom, and now it was his job to pass that wisdom on to others, to ensure that the balance of the natural world was respected and preserved.

In time, Finn began to gather a small group of followers—people who shared his passion for protecting the forest and who wanted to learn how to live in harmony with the land. Together, they traveled to the edges of the Eternal Forest, where they built a small settlement, a place where they could live and work in balance with the natural world.

They called themselves the Keepers of the Forest.

Their mission was simple: to protect the forest, to preserve its magic, and to pass down its wisdom to future generations. They built their homes from the wood of fallen trees, planted gardens filled with native plants, and worked to ensure that the ley lines remained strong and uncorrupted.

Finn became the leader of the Keepers, guiding them with the knowledge he had gained from his time in the forest. But he was not their only teacher. The Phoenix visited them often, her fiery wings lighting up the sky as she shared her wisdom of renewal and rebirth. The Faeries flitted through the trees, their laughter a constant reminder of the joy and wonder that the forest held. And the Guardian of the Forest, though rarely seen, remained a watchful presence, ensuring that the balance of the forest was maintained.

As the years passed, the Keepers of the Forest grew in number, their settlement becoming a thriving community of people dedicated to preserving the legacy of the Eternal Forest. Children were born into the settlement, raised with the stories of the forest's magic, taught to respect the natural world and to live in harmony with it.

And through it all, Finn remained their guide, their storyteller, the one who had brought the legend of the Eternal Forest to the outside world.

The Legend Lives On

Many years later, long after Finn had first set foot in the Eternal Forest, he stood once again at the edge of the Sacred Grove, his hair streaked with silver and his face lined with the marks of time. The forest had changed little in all those years—it remained as beautiful, as mysterious, and as powerful as it had always been.

The Phoenix, now an old friend, landed beside him, her wings glowing softly in the twilight. "You've done well," she said, her voice filled with pride. "The forest is safe, and its story lives on. The balance has been restored, and it will endure for generations to come."

Finn smiled, his heart filled with gratitude for the journey he had taken. He had come to the forest as a traveler, but he was leaving it as something more—a protector, a storyteller, a keeper of the forest's legacy.

"The story will continue to be told," Finn said, his voice steady and filled with certainty. "The lessons of the Eternal Forest will not be forgotten. They will live on, in the hearts of those who come after me."

And as the sun set over the forest, casting its golden light over the treetops, Finn knew that the legend of the Eternal Forest would endure.

It would be passed down through the generations, a story of magic, of balance, of unity, and of hope. And through that story, the wisdom of the forest would continue to guide and inspire those who listened, ensuring that the Eternal Forest—and the world it protected—would never be forgotten.

Don't miss out!

Visit the website below and you can sign up to receive emails whenever Patrick William Lee publishes a new book. There's no charge and no obligation.

https://books2read.com/r/B-A-FLRYB-FNPIF

BOOKS 2 READ

Connecting independent readers to independent writers.

About the Author

Patrick William Lee is a renowned author celebrated for his enchanting tales of magic and wonder. Specializing in the genres of fairy tales, folk tales, legends, and mythology, Patrick weaves stories that transport readers to fantastical realms where the impossible becomes reality. With a deep love for folklore and a talent for crafting timeless narratives, his books captivate the imaginations of readers young and old. When he's not writing, Patrick enjoys exploring ancient forests, studying mythical creatures, and sharing his passion for storytelling with audiences around the world. His works continue to inspire and delight, leaving a lasting impact on the world of literature.